aHunter4Trust

By

Cynthia A Clement

Cover designed by RomCon® www.romcon.com

Cover Image: Deposit Photo,
www.depositphotos.com

Dedication

To my Readers.
Thank you for your patience and support of the aHunter4Hire series.

A special thanks to Jan Carol Abney, Kim Barrows, and John for editing,
proofreading, and inspiration.

Chapter 1

Darrogh was caught between two worlds, Cygnus, where he had been bred, and Earth, the planet he was stranded on. Order and rules were a necessary part of his existence and now they were gone. It was a struggle to live in a place where the tenets that he followed were contrary to the laws of Earth. Despite this, he would never betray his training.

It meant that he was a fugitive on both planets.

Darrogh was a Hunter.

Hunters were an elite race of warriors that had been bred and genetically modified to fight and obey the Kaladin. Civil war had ripped his planet apart. When the ruling class of the Kaladin had been defeated by the Holman, an extinction order had been issued to eradicate all Hunters. Darrogh had been aboard the last prison ship to leave Cygnus.

All other Hunters had gone obediently to their death. It had almost been a complete genocide until the leader of their unit, Ardal, had allowed them to fight so that they could die with honor. They had overtaken the ship, killed their captors, and crash-landed on Earth.

That had been a year ago.

Now, instead of fighting for the Kaladin, Hunters fought for justice on Earth. That often meant they were at odds with the laws of this planet and were fugitives. It was a world that had no respect for honor or the Sacred Code that a Hunter lived by. Earth's atmosphere also played havoc with their perception and body. They were stronger, faster, and their senses were heightened.

Darrogh did not trust Earth's influence on him.

He remained vigilant against the temptations of this planet.

Hunters might carry the same genes as humans, but genetic manipulation and training made them different. Humans were often seduced by pleasure and power. They did not understand the need for caution or believe that their lives might be in danger. Instead, they blindly pursued money and the luxury it bought. The room that he and his team had been led into was a good example of the seductive lure of wealth.

Black leather chairs and couches were placed in front of a silvery marble fireplace. White cabinets and shelves lined the wall surrounding the hearth, and a luxurious Persian rug was centered on a dark oak floor. At the far end was a large bay window that looked across the road to a private park for the owners of the houses in this block. At the other end was a mahogany baby grand piano.

It was the quiet elegance that only the very rich could afford.

Wealth had brought danger, though.

There was a need for a security team to protect the owner of this beautiful townhouse in the very exclusive Chelsea district of London, England. Darrogh had been sent with a team of five to provide that protection. Their client was Sir Robert Creighton, the owner of Creighton's Bank. The bank had been in existence since the sixteenth century and catered almost exclusively to the very rich and elite of the world.

Sir Robert wanted his daughter guarded.

Miss Creighton, had other ideas.

Sir Robert's daughter had ushered them into her reception room. She was looking at her father with raised eyebrows and an expression of impatience. Sir Robert wasn't deterred from his mission. He brought his daughter close for a hug and then stepped back and motioned for Darrogh to join him.

"This is my daughter, Tamsin." Sir Robert made the introduction. "Tamsin, this is Darrogh. I've hired his team to stay here and keep you safe."

"I don't need bodyguards." Tamsin's voice was melodious and low.

"I have received threats and I want to be certain you are safe." Her father was persistent.

"We agreed that I would live my own life." Tamsin flipped her long dark brown hair over her shoulder. "This is my house. You can't insist that these men stay here."

Her father scowled down at her. "I wouldn't ask if I didn't think it was necessary."

Tamsin shook her head. "No one is interested in me. I keep a low profile and I mind my own business."

"Everything has changed since the fiasco with your wedding. People know who you are." Her father sat and pulled her down beside him. "Do this for me."

"I don't want someone living with me or following me around."

Tamsin looked at Darrogh and a shock of awareness went through him. For a second, he was paralyzed by it. It was as if everything he believed had been turned upside down. Before landing on Earth, he'd never been around women. That had changed and for the past year, he'd met several. He did not think it was right for a Hunter to associate with women, but he had learned to accept their presence.

No woman had affected him like this.

Tamsin was gorgeous. She was petite with dark-brown, shoulder-length hair and deep blue eyes. It was not the first time he had met a beautiful woman. When she looked up at him, he felt as if his world had suddenly narrowed so that she was the only person who existed. The room faded until all he could see was her face. He forced his eyes to look away and the spell was broken.

He would have to keep his distance from this woman.

He did not understand what had just happened. He certainly didn't intend for it to happen again. He did not trust the strange sensation he felt when he looked at Tamsin Creighton. Hunters were forbidden to be with a woman and even though some of his brotherhood had found pair bonds on this planet, he refused to accept it. He was a warrior who'd spent his life fighting on the frontlines and on prison planets. Women had never been a part of his life.

"I'm certain this man is very capable of being my bodyguard." Tamsin's voice had a slight waver. "I just don't want him or his team in my house."

"He's staying." Her father clasped one of her hands in his. "This is the only thing that will ease my mind. I would never forgive myself if something happened to you."

Tamsin shook her head. "There are too many of them. Where would they stay?"

"You have more than enough room." Her father's voice was coaxing. "I don't ask for much, but this is something I won't budge on. From what I've read, these men are the best."

Tamsin sighed and looked back at Darrogh. "I don't want you here."

Darrogh nodded. "We will leave."

"No." Sir Robert's voice was sharp. "I'm the one employing you and I insist you stay. If Tamsin won't have you in her house, then you'll have to do it from outside. I want my daughter protected day and night."

Darrogh had learned that humans loved to be contrary. If Sir Robert wanted them to watch her from afar, then they would do so. It would be easier if they could be beside her at all times, yet protection from a distance was not impossible. He had succeeded on far more complicated missions.

"We will start immediately."

"You can't have these men trailing after me and it would look ridiculous if they camped outside of my house." Tamsin's voice rose in protest. "The neighbors would never understand."

"Then let them stay with you." Her father's voice was low. "This is the only way that I'll be at peace."

Tamsin looked at her father and then back at Darrogh. She looked him up and down before glancing over at the rest of his team. Darrogh considered all of them excellent warriors, with skills varied enough to be effective on a mission such as this.

"Do you promise to stay out of my way?"

"As much as possible."

"I don't want you telling me that I can't go places either."

Darrogh nodded. "As you wish."

"And if I decide that I don't want your services anymore, you will leave?"

"Yes."

"I'll expect you to tell me though," Sir Robert interjected. "I want a daily report on my daughter's safety also."

Darrogh nodded.

"I'll let them stay Dad, but this is the last time." Tamsin turned to her father. "I'm old enough to take care of myself. You can't control my life anymore."

"You need protection." Sir Robert stood and pulled his daughter up beside him. "I wouldn't insist otherwise."

Tamsin sighed. "That doesn't make it any easier. Let me walk you out. It's going to take a bit of juggling to get these men settled in here."

Her father chuckled. "Your house is big enough for a family of eight. When you bought it I had hopes you meant to fill it with children. Now I just want to make certain you are safe."

Their voice faded away as they walked out of the room and down the hall to the front door. Darrogh looked around and started to assess the security needs. The large windows would make it difficult to secure. Shutting the drapes would help. It was a townhouse, so there were only windows at the ends of the house. He could see the rear where the kitchen and dining room were. That would be a security nightmare. Those rooms were floor to ceiling glass.

Tamsin came back a few minutes later.

She scowled at Darrogh. "My father is overly protective. I'm not happy about having you here."

"You have made that clear." Darrogh gave a slight bow of the head. "I am the team leader and I will be making all of the decisions concerning your security."

"As long as I agree." Tamsin looked at the other men. "You'd better introduce your team."

Darrogh motioned for the men to step forward one at a time. "This is Firbin. He is our explosive's expert."

"Surely we won't be needing his expertise?" Tamsin's eyes widened.

"He has many other skills." Darrogh moved on to the next man. "This is Jehon. He is adept with equipment and weapons. Next is Breanon. He is an expert marksman. Kerm has the most experience with this area of the world and last is Savis. He is our computer's expert."

Tamsin frowned after the men had been introduced. "You all look similar with your dark hair and eyes. You could be brothers."

"We are brothers in the sense that we are all Hunters."

Darrogh's respect for Tamsin grew. She was observant and that would help with their protection. She was also a woman who understood how to command and negotiate. This was the first woman he'd been assigned to guard. He was impressed with her abilities.

"So you're ex-military." Tamsin shook her head. "I must be crazy to have let my father talk me into this. Follow me and I'll show you where you can sleep. Did you bring a vehicle?"

"No." Darrogh motioned to Jehon. "We will get what we need today. Is there a place to park it?"

"I have parking on the street behind the house. I only have my car, so there is room for one more vehicle."

"Good. Jehon will take care of that now." Darrogh nodded to Jehon, who left the room. "I would also like to set up surveillance outside."

"Is that necessary?"

"Your father insisted that your life was in danger. We need to be thorough."

"My father overreacts." Tamsin's voice was dry. "He also likes to spy on me. I won't tolerate you feeding him any information about me."

Darrogh gave her a searching look. She was serious about fearing her father's motives. He did not know the exact nature of the threat against her, only that her father was paying a lot of money for them to provide protection. Darrogh intended to make certain that she was safe.

"I have no intention of spying on you." Darrogh's voice was low. "It is my duty to protect you and I will do that with my life."

Chapter 2

"I would never expect someone to die for me."

A shiver of awareness went through Tamsin as she focused her gaze on the giant standing in front of her. She looked away and ignored the sensation. She didn't need a man in her life, especially not one that her father was employing.

"Nevertheless, I will." Darrogh's sincerity resonated in his voice. "As will all of my team. It will be an honor to serve you."

Tamsin glanced at the rest of the men in the room. They didn't deny Darrogh's words. She inhaled a sharp breath and turned back to their leader. Stopping her father's interference in her life was going to be more difficult than she'd imagined. Usually he came up with some innocuous excuse to visit, or have his assistant, Henry, accompany her somewhere.

Hiring bodyguards was new.

And what bodyguards.

They all stood over six feet tall, with broad shoulders and muscles bulging beneath their brown camo military-styled jackets and tight-fitting jeans. These men looked prepared to battle an army. Darrogh, their leader, looked tougher than the rest. She would hate to face him in a battle. She didn't know where her father had found these men, but they would instill fear and respect wherever they went.

"What did my father tell you was the threat against me?"

"He did not say." Darrogh looked to the man he'd introduced as Savis. "Show Miss Creighton the video we received."

Savis opened a computer and clicked on a site. It was an email with a video attachment. It was sent from her father's private email address and the video opened onto her father's face. He was leaning close to the computer screen and his voice was low.

"I need help protecting my daughter. I don't know who is threatening her. She isn't safe and your website said that you would help as long as my concerns were sincere and true. I understand the penalty if I lie, but I swear I am telling you the truth. I will pay you whatever you need. Please protect my daughter."

Tamsin was shocked by the intense fear in her father's voice. "What happens if he lied?"

"He will die." Darrogh spoke without hesitation.

Tamsin gasped. "You can't kill him for lying."

"He knew the risks when he contacted us." Darrogh's gaze didn't waver from her. "I believe Sir Robert thinks your life is in danger. It would be foolish to ignore his concerns."

Her father had done some outrageous things in the past, but never something like this. To risk death so that he could control her life was extreme. If she knew her father, he had a backup plan. He'd probably hired a lawyer to get him out of the deal. She would have loved to see the lawyer's face when he found out the penalty for breaking the contract was death.

Tamsin forced herself to be serious. If it was a matter of her father's life, she could put up with these men for a while. First, she wanted to insure that he would be safe.

"If I let you guard me, my father won't be killed?"

Darrogh hesitated a second before he replied. "We must be certain that there is a danger."

"Isn't it enough that my father believes that my life is at risk?"

Darrogh nodded. "I believe your father is sincere."

"I'll bet this is tied up with Creighton's." Tamsin tried to keep the bitterness from her voice. "He'd do anything to make certain his precious bank was safe."

"It is you he wants protected." Savis clicked on another email. "He is paying a lot of money to hire our services."

Tamsin looked at the figure.

It was one million pounds.

Her father easily had that much money and plenty more. To pay that to a security team was ludicrous, though. She considered the possibility that there was a real threat against her and then she dismissed it. Her father wanted only one thing and that was for Tamsin to reconcile with Winchester Nethercott.

"He wants me to marry my ex-fiancé." Tamsin didn't hide her contempt. "I've already refused. I won't have you trying to change my mind."

"A woman makes her own decisions about her mate." Darrogh frowned. "A man has no say in this. Why would we force you to marry someone?"

"Because you're working for my father." Tamsin threw the challenge out. "With the kind of money he has paid you, you'd be obligated to do what he wanted."

"We are warriors, not matchmakers."

Kerm stepped forward. "I am more familiar with the traditions in this country than Darrogh. I understand your concerns. Darrogh speaks the truth. We are here only to protect."

Tamsin glanced at all of the men. They seemed sincere enough and except for their leader Darrogh, she felt comfortable with them. It wouldn't take them long to realize that she wasn't in danger and then they'd leave.

"You can stay, but remember, if I ask you to leave, you go."

"Of course." Darrogh nodded. "We will obey your wishes. Now I need to secure this house so that we are aware of everyone who comes and goes."

"That shouldn't take you too long." Tamsin walked to the window. "I'm the only one who lives here, and I seldom go out during the day except to the park."

"Two men will accompany you."

Tamsin rolled her eyes. What a sight that would be. Two gorgeous giants walking beside her. The neighbors would immediately suspect something was wrong. Perhaps the park wasn't such a good idea.

"What happens when I go clubbing?"

"Clubbing?" Darrogh's voice held confusion.

"It is a term for going out and partying," Kerm said.

Darrogh nodded. "Is this at a private house?"

"It's at a nightclub. I'm a member of several and if my father insists on knowing my actions, I think I should give you something to report back to him."

"Your father has not asked us to tell him your movements," Darrogh said. "I need more information about your nighttime activity. Are there many people at these clubs?"

"Hundreds."

"Then we would need to setup surveillance outside and accompany you inside." Darrogh's voice was serious. "We are a large team. We will be able to guard you no matter where you choose to go."

Tamsin grinned. "I might take you up on that challenge."

She couldn't let these men or her father interfere with her life. Since she'd freed herself from her engagement to Winchester Nethercott and her father's dynastic dreams, she'd been able to make her own decisions about her future. That future didn't include being bound by the demands of Creighton's Bank. Even though the bank had been in the family for centuries, she didn't want the burden of continuing the traditions. She wanted to use her knowledge to make a difference in the world.

She wouldn't allow her father's concerns to destroy her plans.

When she'd turned twenty-five she had gained access to her trust fund and started to invest on her own. Soon she would see her dream of a bank that made a difference, come to fruition. Her father didn't know what she'd done. As far as he was concerned she'd wasted the last year with partying and spending money. She'd guarded her privacy to ensure that nothing would stop her from her goal.

"So we are clear on the rules." Tamsin raised her hand and folded her fingers as she made each point. "You do not spy on me. You do not report my activities to my father. You do not interfere in my life. This is my house. You don't question my actions."

Darrogh crossed his arms over his chest.

A fission of doubt went through Tamsin. He was a formidable opponent and it might have been a mistake to challenge him. For several seconds there was silence and then she noticed a gleam of approval in his gaze.

"I respect a woman who knows how to command." Darrogh's voice held admiration. "I am a Hunter and am bound by the Sacred Code. My team and I will abide by your commands except where your safety is concerned."

Tamsin released the breath she'd been holding. "I have your word."

"As long as you understand that if you are in danger, we will act as necessary."

Tamsin glanced at the rest of the men. They were as serious as Darrogh. She didn't believe for a minute that she was in peril. Her father had dreamed up this ploy to gain access to her life. What did it matter? It couldn't hurt to humor him as long as these men abided by her rules.

Tamsin held out her hand to Darrogh. "We have a deal."

Darrogh looked down at her outstretched hand and paused before taking it in his. A jolt of electricity passed through her. It felt as if energy passed from Darrogh to her. There was a whisper of sensation at the back of her head and then it was gone. She inhaled a sharp breath and looked up at him.

Darrogh scowled and released her hand as if she'd burned him.

Whatever had happened, he'd felt it too.

Tamsin straightened her shoulders and turned to the rest of the men. She'd have to be more careful around Darrogh. She didn't understand what had passed between them and she had no intention of finding out. Keeping her distance from him was the best solution.

"I'll show you where you can sleep." She forced her voice to remain steady.

"We will not need much space." Darrogh's tone was gruff. "We will guard in shifts."

"I'll put you all up on the top floor." She headed toward the stairs. "It's an open space, with a couple of futons. If you need more beds, then you'll have to use the bedrooms downstairs."

When they reached the third floor she led them into the open area. There was a bathroom with a shower, closets, soft carpeting on the floor, and three futons that were set up as a seating area. The previous owners had used the space for a playroom and Tamsin had kept the space open. On the right side of the stairs was another room that was unfurnished.

Tamsin opened the door of the spare room. "If you need extra space we can arrange to have a bed put into this room."

Darrogh stepped close and peered into the empty room. Tamsin's heart started to beat fast and she gripped the door handle tighter. Her breath caught in her throat and she had to force herself to remain beside him.

"We will set up our controls here." Darrogh moved away.

"There is a control room in the basement. That's where the house's security system is installed."

Darrogh glanced at Savis. "Will that be sufficient?"

"I will connect into the system." Savis clasped a black backpack and headed down the stairs.

"These arrangements are more than adequate. Firbin and Kerm will set our gear up here. Breanon will scout the outside." The men did as Darrogh asked and then he turned to her. "I need to see where you sleep."

"I sleep alone." Tamsin's voice rose. "No one is guarding me there."

"As you wish." A nerve twitched in Darrogh's jaw. "I want to make certain that the room is secure. We will guard you from the outside at night."

Tamsin shut the spare door with a quiet click. "I overreacted. I apologize."

"There is no need." Darrogh followed her down the stairs. "I would never intrude on your personal space unless you were in danger."

Tamsin paused on the landing to the first floor. "I have your word on that?"

"You have my vow."

Tamsin would have to accept that. She walked into the master retreat. It took up the whole first floor with a bedroom, ensuite, sitting room, and a private outdoor terrace. She'd decorated it in muted tones of cream, beige and slate gray. It was her sanctuary and the one place she could relax in. She waited while Darrogh looked into each room, testing the locks on the windows and walking out onto the terrace. He was there for several minutes before coming inside.

"I would like to set up camera surveillance on the terrace," Darrogh said. "I'll have a man on the roof at all times too."

"Is that necessary?"

"Yes." Darrogh's voice was firm.

"My father thinks I can't take care of myself. He's wrong."

Darrogh nodded. "I understand your concerns. Every man of my team is committed to protecting you. We will keep you safe. You have no need to be worried."

Tamsin raised an eyebrow. "The only reason I'm allowing you to stay is because my father insisted. I have no intention of relying on you for my safety. I trust no man."

Chapter 3

It had been a week since Darrogh and his team had accepted the assignment of guarding Tamsin Creighton. She still did not trust their motives and she made no secret of that fact. Every night they had followed her from one play spot to the next. Tonight was no different. They were in Beauvie's, an exclusive, members-only London nightclub.

Colored strobe lights flashed to the beat of ear-shattering music.

Bodies crowded the floor, gyrating to the deafening noise.

It reminded him of the battlefield. The only thing missing was the smell of death. He did not understand humans. Why would they deliberately reproduce the sights and sounds of the frontlines of a war zone? Was it because they liked warfare or was it just a coincidence? Whatever the reason, the constant barrage of stimuli had his senses on full alert.

Darrogh's eyes narrowed as he focused on Tamsin. Her name was a constant litany in his head. He could not ignore the effect she had on him, but he was stronger than his fellow Hunters. He would not succumb to the lure of a woman. It was forbidden. A Hunter had no right being near women, much less feeling a connection to one. Some of the warriors in his unit had found mates, but he did not believe in the legends.

She moved in and out of the flailing bodies as she made her way to the long steel bar at the edge of the dance floor. She was a vision of grace and poise in a short red dress that hugged her curves. Darrogh inhaled a quick breath and followed.

She did not want him near.

He ignored her rejection.

Her protection was his job and he had never failed a mission before. She would not be the first to underestimate his abilities as a warrior. He reached her side and stood a step behind her. It was right and fitting for a Hunter to show deference to a woman. Despite customs being different on this planet, he had sworn to live and die by the Hunter's code. Nothing would change that.

"Leave me alone."

Her voice sent a frisson of heat through him.

Darrogh ignored the sensation.

"I cannot. My mission is to protect you."

"I'm not in danger here."

She swirled around and glared at him. Blue eyes flashed and even in the darkened club, Darrogh could see her wariness. Her reaction to him was always the same. It was not his place to judge her behavior, but he had observed that this was how she treated most of the men she encountered, except her father.

"Your safety is my concern."

Darrogh kept his voice neutral. He had spent his life fighting among men on the frontlines and was used to barking orders. Since arriving on Earth, he had come to learn that women did not respond to the same tone of voice as men did.

"It's a waste of time." She turned back to the bartender and waited until he presented her with a concoction of frothy pink liquid. She took a couple of sips before turning to face him. "I don't know how you expect anyone to hurt me in this place."

"There are enough people here to do harm."

Tamsin took a step closer to him and looked up into his face. She was a tiny woman, barely reaching his shoulders. She stood near enough that he could smell the exotic perfume she was wearing and feel the brush of her breath against his neck.

"And enough witnesses to ensure that they wouldn't get away." Tamsin pushed a finger into his chest. "My father's worries are not mine. In case you haven't noticed, I don't live by his rules anymore."

Darrogh glanced around the nightclub. It was a scene of constant motion and lights, a stark contrast to the elegance and quiet of Tamsin's residence. Every day she spent in quiet seclusion at home, only to leave it for the noise and confusion of the nightclubs. Even though she laughed and danced, Darrogh sensed it was an act. He did not know if it was for his team's or her father's benefit.

"To live by another's rules can be a burden." Darrogh looked down into Tamsin's deep blue eyes, fighting the temptation to succumb to their lure. "That does not mean those rules are not necessary."

Tamsin opened her mouth to speak and then shut it. She continued to stare at him for several seconds before glancing away. "Have it your way. I'm going to the Ladies' Room. Don't follow me."

She took another gulp of her drink before handing it to him and walking away. Darrogh clenched his jaw. He was a warrior, not a servant. He had never had a charge who fought his security before. Tamsin might not think his protection was necessary, but her father did. He took a step forward and then stopped.

His presence only antagonised her.

She treated the rest of the team with relaxed tolerance.

"Firbin, follow her. She has gone to the Ladies' Room."

The ease of being able to mind connect with his fellow warriors was a relief on a mission like this. It would have been impossible to hear each other with all the noise and chaos of the nightclub. It was not the first time it had been a tactical advantage, and that was why it was a closely guarded secret among Hunters. Firbin was the youngest of their unit. He had taken to life on this planet quicker than the rest of them and had an ease of interaction with humans that Darrogh would never have.

"Did she refuse your protection again?" Firbin's words held a hint of curiosity.

"Yes." Honesty between warriors was necessary for survival. *"My presence is unwelcome."*

"She thinks you hover."

"How do you know this?"

There were a few seconds of silence before Firbin answered. *"She told Jehon."*

The fact that Tamsin had spoken to Jehon about their protection was the first sign that she was accepting their presence. The soldier in him knew that he could use this to make their security more effective.

"When did she communicate this?" Darrogh's tone was clipped.

"Before we entered this place. You were still with the vehicle. I did not think it was important." Firbin's voice held regret. *"We would have told you at the debriefing this evening."*

"I can use this information to keep her safe now."

"She is not pleased with your commands."

"A warrior does not take words personally. Survival depends on knowing everything, no matter how small."

"I have located Tamsin. She is exiting the restroom."

"Keep close." Darrogh's eyes strained through the crowd, searching until he spotted her. *"If she prefers your company, then you can guard her tonight."*

"It will be done."

Darrogh watched Firbin take his place behind Tamsin. The tightness in his chest still did not ease. He should be pleased that he had found a way to overcome her reluctance to having them guard her. Instead, his anxiety increased. His eyes scanned the overcrowded dance floor before looking up at the second-floor balcony that surrounded the main floor.

It seemed as crowded as the main floor. Patrons were leaning over the railing with drinks in their hands and fingers pointed down below to the dancers. The crowds alone made this place difficult to provide protection. Add in the low lighting and flashes of strobes, and it was a nightmare. Darrogh's only consolation was that it would be just as difficult for someone to abduct Tamsin from here as it was to protect her.

He refused to let his thoughts linger on Tamsin's harsh criticism. He had sensed since their first meeting that she was not comfortable with him. Her father's insistence that she was in danger had not changed her attitude toward his security detail. She wanted them to leave her alone.

She was a woman.

Hunters obeyed women.

Tamsin was human and unused to the ways of commanding warriors. He could not trust her to make the right decision. He did not even trust her to stay with them. She tried to escape their protection at least once a day. Today had been an easy one until they had come to her favorite night spot.

Tamsin had been unusually compliant. She had not once tried to escape. He glanced around the floor searching for her, breathing a sigh of relief when he caught sight of her beside Firbin. She was leaning close and laughing, something she had never done with him.

Darrogh crossed his arms and turned away. He did not want her to treat him like the others. He was in charge of the team and he needed to maintain control of the operation. If Tamsin was too friendly with him, he might be tempted to bend the rules. That could only lead to one thing. She would slip away from their protection and be at risk.

Her father, Sir Robert Creighton, was paying a lot of money to have his daughter protected, and it was his job to stop any harm happening to Tamsin. It did not matter that she did not cooperate. He had seen enough combat to know how to defeat obstacles.

Darrogh continued to survey the patrons in the club for the next half hour. Every few minutes he would locate Tamsin and ascertain that she was safe. He had just finished another assessment of the front entrance and dance floor when a familiar twinge of apprehension stopped him.

A tingle of unease raced up his spine.

It was a sensation he had not felt in over a year. In the past, the feeling had warned him of danger. He had learned never to ignore it because it had saved his life more than once.

"*Jehon, do you have anything unusual happening at the door?*"

"*People are still arriving.*" Jehon answered immediately.

"*Breanon report.*"

Breanon was doing surveillance outside. He was on the roof of a building across the street with a rifle trained on the road. He was one of the best marksmen in their unit. If anyone tried to snatch Tamsin his orders were to shoot them dead. The Sacred Code was very clear that there was only one outcome for someone doing harm to a woman. Death.

"*Cars are still arriving with guests. None of them are gaining access. They are lining up outside the building.*"

The knot of disquiet had settled in his stomach.

"*Firbin take Tamsin out of the club.*"

He headed toward Firbin. He would feel better once he was certain Tamsin was safe. She would be upset over his orders to leave, but he could not risk ignoring his gut. Something was not right about this place. He needed to get her to safety.

"*She has gone into the restroom again.*"

"*Go after her.*" Darrogh bit the words out. "*We need to leave immediately.*"

"*It is restricted to women.*" Firbin's voice held a note of horror. "*It is wrong to invade a woman's space.*"

"I'll do it." Darrogh had reached Firbin's side. There was no longer any need to mind connect. "How long has she been there?"

"Ten minutes."

"Prepare to leave as soon as I come out with her."

Darrogh opened the door that led to the Ladies' Room and found himself in a long hallway. There were several doors on one side and one at the end of the hall. The knot in his stomach grew tighter.

He pushed the door labeled Ladies' Room open and was greeted by several shrieking women.

He ignored them.

"Tamsin."

There was no answer.

He went down the long row of stalls and pounded on the doors. Only two were occupied, and neither one by Tamsin. He turned back to the group of outraged women clustered at the sinks.

"Did a woman with long, dark hair and a short, red dress come in?"

"I'm a sucker for the tall, dark, and jealous act." A blonde woman in her early twenties staggered toward him. "Will I do?"

Darrogh clenched his jaw. "Have you seen her?"

"Have it your way." The girl shrugged. "She came in and then left again."

"How long ago."

"Ten minutes, maybe more." The girl looked back at her friends and they nodded.

"She was not seen leaving."

The girl giggled. "I guess she used the escape door."

"Where is this door?"

"It's at the end of the hallway." One of the women leaning against a sink answered. "Every club has one. You never know when you'll have to evade a possessive man's attention."

Darrogh ignored the laughter behind him as he left the room. He rushed down the hallway and pushed open the escape door. Stairs led down to an alley between the buildings. Tamsin was not in sight. If she had left this way, then they would have difficulty locating her. This door was locked from the outside so they had never considered it an access point for an assailant. He went back into the club and stopped beside Firbin.

"Has she come out?"

Firbin shook his head.

"Was she talking with anyone before she left you?"

"There was a tall, dark-haired man that she seemed to know. They were chatting for several minutes before he left the club."

"You are certain of this?"

"Yes." Firbin's tone was clipped. "What is the problem?"

Darrogh started to the door. "Tamsin has escaped."

"She has probably returned to her house." Firbin kept pace beside him. "She had been complaining about the noise."

"Perhaps." Darrogh motioned for Jehon to follow them outside. "I need access to the CCTV cameras on this street and the alley between these two buildings."

"Savis can access the feed," Jehon said as they were joined by Kerm.

"Take Firbin with you. We are looking for a dark-haired man that she was last seen speaking with."

"We will find him." Jehon's tone was brisk.

"Get all of the details and then destroy the feed. We do not want the authorities following her." Darrogh watched the two men walk across the street to where their cube van was parked. It contained their weapons and equipment, and the last man of their team, Savis, their communications and computer expert.

Darrogh walked to the alley where Tamsin had escaped. Kerm followed. It smelled of urine and rotting food. Trash containers lined the wall, and refuse littered the pavement. His stomach clenched at the thought of Tamsin walking through this filth. He would have taken her anywhere she wanted. Why was it so difficult for her to accept his protection?

"There is only one entrance to this alley." Kerm pointed to the fence that blocked the laneway at the opposite end.

Darrogh looked up. "There's a security camera on the opposite building. Access it and meet us back at the van."

Kerm nodded and left.

The knot in Darrogh's stomach tightened.

It was possible Tamsin had just gone home, yet his senses said different. He did not want to examine how he knew. Ever since he had accepted this mission he had been aware of a link with Tamsin. He hoped it was only this planet's effect on him because he refused to consider what else it could be. Whatever the reason for his connection, he knew one thing for certain.

Tamsin was in danger.

Chapter 4

She was free.

A rush of adrenaline raced through Tamsin as she fought the urge to shout with glee. After a week of constant surveillance, she had finally escaped the suffocating presence of the men her father had hired to watch her. She didn't care what excuse they gave, she knew it was just one more of her father's tactics to control her life.

Darrogh's image flashed through her mind. She envisioned the familiar scowl on his face when he learned that she'd escaped. He insisted that she was in danger. Several times during the past week she had almost let herself trust him, until she remembered.

Men lied.

Darrogh wasn't like any man she'd met.

He seemed more concerned with her safety than spying on her. She'd been dragging his team to every obnoxious and loud nightclub in the city of London for the past several evenings, and they never voiced any objections. It was as if they expected her to do outrageous things. She shook the thought from her mind and ran down the fire escape.

She could take care of herself.

George said he'd bring his car to the entrance of the alley and then drive her home. She almost reeled from the stench of the laneway, bringing her hand up to cover her nose and mouth. She quickened her pace. When she saw an electric-blue Mercedes AMG pull into the lane she ran.

Her ride was here.

George Saxby was a couple of years older than her. They'd been in the same class at the London School of Economics. He was the epitome of tall, dark, and handsome, with intense brown eyes and a smile that had charmed many of their fellow classmates.

George grinned as she opened the passenger door and slid in. "Do you like my car?"

"Very much." Tamsin put her seatbelt on. "You always said you'd get a fancy sports car when you were making money."

"It impresses the women." George reversed and headed down the street.

Tamsin rolled her eyes. "You haven't changed. When are you going to settle down?"

"Never." George shifted gears and the vehicle lurched forward. "I enjoy a different woman every night."

"That's why I never dated you." Tamsin leaned back into the soft-leather seat. "It would have spoiled our friendship."

"Is that what we were, friends?" George's voice was low. "I thought you couldn't stand the sight of me."

Tamsin inhaled a sharp breath. "Why would you say that? We hung out with the same group of people."

"You avoided me whenever possible."

A shiver of warning raced through her and settled into a knot in her stomach. She'd been so happy to see a familiar face that she'd forgotten how George's intense stares had made her uncomfortable in the past. There had been rumors about his rough behavior with women. No one had come out and accused him of anything, but she'd avoided him. So many years had passed since then. It was ridiculous to still harbor doubts about him.

"I thought you were too busy being the big man around campus to notice me."

"I noticed." George's voice was wry. "Are you going to tell me what all the cloak and dagger stuff was back there?"

"My dad is having me followed." The tension eased from Tamsin. "I had to get away, even if it was only for an hour."

"Are they likely to pursue us?"

"They'll try. It'll take hours for them to figure it out." Tamsin glanced out the window. They were not driving in the direction of her house. "I thought you were going to drive me home."

"After you have a drink at my place." George turned to her with a lopsided smile. "For old time's sake."

Tamsin hesitated. All she wanted was to be alone. Still, she'd dragged George into this crazy escapade so the least she could do was have a drink.

"You'll take me home afterwards?"

"I promise." George down shifted and turned a corner. They were in an area of Knightsbridge that she didn't recognize. It was an upscale neighborhood. George stopped at a converted brick warehouse and pulled through a garage door that led to an underground parking area. There were no other cars there.

Tamsin frowned. "Where are your neighbors?"

"I own the building." George shut the car off. "I like my privacy."

It was a large building and the square footage must be massive. "Do you live in the whole place?"

"I'm renovating." George opened his door and waited for Tamsin to exit the car. "When I have a flat ready, then I'll consider renting."

"You must have a fortune tied up in this project." Tamsin followed George to the lift. "You've done well for yourself."

"I had to." George held the door open for her. "I wasn't born with money."

"Trust me, it can be a curse." Tamsin leaned against the elevator wall. "My father is always worried about what will happen to the bank once he dies."

"I thought you worked at Creighton's."

"Not since I called off my wedding."

The lift stopped and Tamsin waited for George to exit, before she followed. They walked into a small hallway with a door across from the elevator, which he held open for her. He switched on the lights as they entered a large converted loft at the top of the building. Windows spanned the height of the south-facing wall, giving a spectacular view of the city-scape. The rest of the area was divided into kitchen, dining, and living space. There was a partition wall on the north side and Tamsin assumed this was for the bedrooms and bathrooms. Everything was done in black and white, with an accent color of red.

"It's wonderful." Tamsin walked to the windows. "No wonder you don't want to share this with others."

"It's an investment for my future." George stopped beside her.

"So you plan on selling it one day."

Tamsin did a quick calculation in her head. George would walk away with millions. He'd been one of the best students at university and it was easy to see that he had translated that knowledge into action. She'd been quietly investing herself. She might ask George for advice about some of her slower growth projects and maybe even about the real estate market.

"What would you like to drink?" George walked over to the island that divided the living space from kitchen.

"White wine, if you have it." Tamsin turned back to the city view, watching the reflection of George in the windows as he uncorked a bottle of wine. He spun around and took two glasses from the cupboard. When he turned back he had two full goblets of wine in his hands.

"Let's get comfortable." He walked over to a black couch and put her wine on the coffee-table. "It's been a few years since school."

Tamsin took a seat opposite George on a matching leather chair. "Some things are the same. We're both single."

"I heard about your engagement. The papers were full of speculation after you called the wedding off."

"A slow news day." Tamsin took a gulp of the wine. It had a bitter aftertaste.

George raised an eyebrow. "Are you going to tell me why?"

"It was the usual story." Tamsin put her glass back on the table. "I couldn't trust him."

"You caught him with someone else." George shook his head. "He was a fool."

"Not unique though."

Tamsin kicked her heels off and curled her legs under her. She reached for her wine and took another sip. She scrunched her nose at the taste and put it back down. She couldn't say much for George's wine choice.

"Nethercott has never been known as the settling down sort. Why marry him?"

"It's what my father wanted." Tamsin pushed her hair behind her ears. "Enough about me. Tell me what you've been doing. From the looks of this place, you've been very successful since uni."

"I'm a VP at Jefferson and Woodcroft's."

Tamsin was impressed. Jefferson and Woodcroft's were the leading stockbrokers in the country. No wonder George was able to sit on this building and not rent any of the flats out. He must be making millions a year and that was before bonuses.

"It looks like I should be coming to you for financial advice."

George laughed. "Your family owns one of the oldest and most respected banks in the country. You hardly need my guidance."

"I don't work for Creighton's anymore."

"You might not work there, but the bank is in your blood." George's tone hardened. "Or are you living off your Trust Fund?"

"I'm between jobs right now."

Tamsin tried to keep her voice neutral. George had never made a secret of the fact that he was disdainful of those who had come from family money. He'd worked jobs after classes to put himself through school.

"I'm glad to see you're not going to let your education go to waste." George gulped down the last of his wine and pointed at her full glass. "Don't you like the Chardonnay?"

"I'm not thirsty." Tamsin looked down at her watch. "It's getting late, George. I appreciate you helping me escape my handlers, and for the chance to get caught up, but I'm tired. I'm going to call a taxi and go home."

"I'll drive you home when we're finished." George stood. "In a few minutes you won't be able to walk on your own."

Uncertainty filled Tamsin. "What are you talking about?"

"I drugged your wine." George's statement was made in a monotone voice.

"That isn't funny." Tamsin gave a half-laugh. "I would have thought you'd outgrown your pranks."

Tamsin put her feet on the ground. She had to hold onto the chair until her head stopped spinning. She'd had one drink at the club and a few sips of wine. She wasn't drunk. She glanced at her glass and a shiver of alarm went through her. She hadn't actually seen George pour the wine. What if he had put something in it?

"I've moved beyond university." George picked up her glass and held it out to her. "You might prefer to finish this. It'll help you forget."

"Why would I want to forget?" Tamsin forced herself to stand. She swayed and it took all of her energy to stay upright.

George shrugged. "Have it your way. Just know that if you say anything about tonight, I'll kill you."

Panic rose in her throat, making it difficult for her to breathe.

The man standing in front of her was a stranger.

"What happened to you?"

"I got smart." George walked to the sink and poured her wine down the drain. "After the first girl reported me, I made sure no one said another word."

"What kind of man are you?"

"I take what I want and I don't apologize." George swung his hands around the loft. "How else do you think I was able to afford this?"

"You worked for it." Tamsin tried to take a step toward the door, but her feet refused to move. She swallowed back her dread. She needed a clear head to get out of this situation and fear would only cloud her judgement.

"If I played by the rules it would have taken me a lifetime to accumulate that much money." George snorted. "Rules are for suckers."

"What about integrity?" Tamsin's words were slurred.

"It's out of place in this day and age." George took a step toward her. She tried to move backwards. Her legs hit the edge of the glass coffee-table. "People only care about themselves."

Tamsin's throat was dry. "We're friends. I would have helped you."

George threw his head back and laughed. "You needed an escape from your bodyguards or you wouldn't have lowered yourself to get into my car."

Tamsin steadied herself with a hand on the back of the chair. "That's not true."

"Isn't it?" George raised an eyebrow. "If I'm such a good friend why wasn't I invited to your wedding? All your high-society pals were on the invitation list, but not your old buddy George."

"Most of the guests were business associates."

"Enough." George shouted. "Fate played into my hands tonight and I mean to take what I want. This is payback for all of the snubs you and your friends gave me over the years."

"You're wrong." Tamsin's eyes widened as George started toward her. There was a look of wildness in his eyes. "What are you going to do?"

"I thought that was obvious." George grabbed her shoulders. "I'm going to have my way with you. I've dreamt of this for years. Everything I would do to and with you, once I had you in my control."

George's grip tightened.

"This is better than I planned." He shook her and threw her back against the chair. "You'll remember every moment and touch."

"I'll scream."

"Go ahead. No one can hear you." George pulled his tie off. "Do you think this is the first time I've had a woman here against her will?"

She forced back her revulsion.

"Do you hate us so much?"

"Quite the opposite." George flung his jacket onto the couch. "The problem is that most woman won't give me what I want. I like it rough. Women are ashamed that pain could give them pleasure and they cry foul."

"So you drug them?"

"It's easier than foreplay." George walked over to a cabinet and opened the doors. His back was to her so she tried to stand. When her legs wouldn't work, she dropped to her knees and crawled. She had barely made it past the living area when George hauled her back by her hair.

Pain screeched through her scalp.

"Where do you think you're going?" He had a video camera in his free hand and he was aiming at her. "It's time for your big shoot."

He pulled her back to the center of the room where a large black area rug covered the floor. He placed her in the center and set up his camera on a tripod before undoing his belt. The sound of him snapping it sent terror and revulsion through Tamsin.

She was helpless.

He brought the belt up to her chin.

"Do you like it rough Tamsin?" His voice sent a chill through her.

She shook her head. "Don't do this."

"I'll take that as a no." He stood up and pulled his shirt off. "That's good. I like it when they try and fight me."

"You're sick."

"Maybe, but you're not going to get out of here alive. You should have finished your wine."

"No." Tamsin throat went dry as the implication of his words became clear. He was going to kill her.

"I can't afford to have women remembering and going to the police." George ran the edge of his belt down her cheek. "That means I can do anything I like to you, and believe me, I have a vivid imagination."

"Let me go and I swear I won't tell anyone what you threatened to do."

"Where would the fun be in that?" George's fingers moved down the bodice of her gown. "Besides, the dead can't speak."

Tamsin struggled to push away. She couldn't feel her feet and when she tried to move, nothing happened. She balled her fingers into a fist and raised her arm to hit George. He laughed.

"Is this what you want to do?" He slapped her face, sending her head reeling backwards.

Pain seared through her.

George grabbed the silk of her dress and yanked. It ripped down the middle, exposing her lace bra underneath. She struggled to cover herself, but her hands refused to obey. Her stomach churned with nausea and a part of her wished she'd drank more of the wine. It was only a fleeting thought. Anger burned through her and she used the last surge of her strength to bring her knee up into George's groin.

He howled in agony before he pulled her up to her knees and dragged her over to the chair. He bent her over the chair arm and pulled her dress up over her shoulders. He pushed her face into the cushion and kept a hand on her neck so that she couldn't move. Every nerve in her body cried out at in outrage over the violation, yet she was powerless to fight.

The image of Darrogh came into her mind.

She swore she could hear his voice reassuring her that he would be there.

He would never have let something like this happen to her. She was in this predicament because she'd put her trust in the wrong man. What a fool she'd been. It was her own fault. She struggled once more to rear her body off the chair. George was too strong for her. There was no escape.

She was going to be violently raped.

Then she'd be murdered.

Chapter 5

Inaction was fueling Darrogh's frustration.

The purr of the van's engine was a constant reminder that they were no closer to finding Tamsin now, than ten minutes ago. They had the CCTV video from the bar and the alley, but no real clue as to where Tamsin had gone.

"There." Savis pointed at his computer.

Darrogh glanced over his shoulder and nodded. "Can you read the license of the vehicle she's getting into?"

"I'm already searching for it." Images were flashing on the screen where Kerm was working. "I'll have an address in a few minutes."

"Good." Darrogh exhaled a breath.

"She has probably gone home." Firbin spoke for the first time since they had entered the van. "She told me she wanted time alone."

Darrogh glanced over at the young warrior and nodded. "I hope you are right."

"We cannot assume that." Savis's voice was low. "We were hired to protect so that means she is in danger from someone. This might be that person."

Darrogh's hands tightened into fists. He had been a soldier too long to rely on things going smoothly. Tamsin was a difficult woman to guard, yet that did not excuse his failure. If she wanted to be alone and escape them, it was because she was uncomfortable with his skills.

The van door opened and Breanon entered. He'd kept his watch across the street until Darrogh was certain that Tamsin was not returning to the Club. There was no doubt that she had left with the man that Firbin had seen her talking to in the Club.

Now they had to find her.

"Firbin, and Jehon go to Tamsin's house." Darrogh turned to the warriors. "If she is there, make certain she stays there."

The men jumped out of the van.

"You believe she is in trouble." Savis's words were a statement.

"My instinct has never been wrong."

"We will find her." Kerm's fingers raced across his keyboard. "A Hunter does not fail."

Darrogh clenched his jaw. "We will have to cover our tracks. If the man she is with has harmed or touched her in any way then he will answer to the Sacred Code."

Breanon reached into the metal box beside him and started pulling weapons out. He checked each pistol for bullets and handed one to Darrogh and Savis. He then rested his rifle across his lap and leaned back against the side of the van.

"I have already cleared the CCTV footage showing us entering the club and Tamsin leaving." Savis turned back to his computer. "There will be no evidence of our presence."

"Good. We need to keep our existence here quiet. There are cameras inside the club. Make certain the footage for tonight is also destroyed."

Savis nodded. "It has been done."

"Got him." Kerm announced. "The vehicle is registered to a George Saxby. He has a flat in Knightsbridge."

"Drive there." Darrogh put his gun into his waistband. "Savis do a search on Mr. Saxby."

"Already started." Savis frowned at his laptop. "He attended the same school as Tamsin. He also works with finances."

Darrogh looked at the picture of the man on the computer screen. He had dark hair and brown eyes, pleasant features that humans would consider handsome. Darrogh did not trust the deadness in his eyes. That might be the trick of the photographer, though.

"Firbin said that she recognized him."

Savis looked up from his computer. "He owns the building where his flat is and I cannot find any other residents there."

"Good." Darrogh held onto his seat as the Kerm pulled away from the curb. "We will not have to worry about witnesses. What about security cameras?"

"I'm searching the database now."

Five minutes later Savis spoke. "I have the vehicle arriving at the address. It is underground parking and I cannot see if she is with him."

"She is there."

Darrogh could feel her in his bones. Her fear and horror were racing through him. He had never connected with another like this before. He hoped it was because this was the first time he had been responsible for a woman's safety. Any other reason was unacceptable to him. Darrogh still followed the rules that had governed his life before landing on Earth.

Women were forbidden to Hunters.

"Knock out the security cameras and the CCTV in the area." Darrogh's voice hardened. "If you cannot see if he has a passenger, then no one else will either."

"Done."

Silence filled the van until Kerm came to a stop.

"Kerm stay here. We will get Tamsin." Darrogh nodded to his men.

They picked up their weapons and exited the vehicle. It was a cool, summer night with only a slight mist in the air. Fog would have given them better cover, but it was not to be. Darrogh led the men to the large warehouse where the car had been seen entering. There was no obvious front entryway, so they made their way along the side. In the rear, there was a large loading dock door.

A computer pad lock was beside it.

Darrogh motioned to Savis who went to the security lock. Within minutes, he had the door opened and they entered the darkened building. It took a couple of seconds to focus their eyes before they could see. It was one of the benefits of this planet. Hunters had already been genetically modified for improved night vision. Earth made it that much better.

There was a lift, and beside it, stairs. Darrogh started up the steps. An elevator would only alert someone to their coming, and surprise was their best weapon. They stopped at the first floor, Savis and Breanon waited with guns ready while Darrogh opened the door. There were construction tools scattered throughout a large open surface.

They exited and moved up to the next landing.

It too was empty.

In total they searched five floors before they came to the sixth. It was the last one in the building. Tamsin had to be here. There were no other places to search. Darrogh leaned against the wall beside the door and took a deep breath. He was just about to open the door when he received a mind connection from Firbin.

"We are at Tamsin's house. She isn't here."

Darrogh closed his eyes for a second before replying. *"We have found the man she left with. We will make certain she is safe."*

Darrogh turned the handle.

They entered a hallway.

There was only one other door and the lift. This was the only floor that had been renovated, so it had to be George Saxby's home. Darrogh looked up, noting the two security cameras on the ceiling. One was aimed at the lift and the other at the door. He signaled to Breanon, who used his rifle to push the cameras up to the ceiling. Darrogh did not want to take the chance that they would be seen coming.

He turned the knob of the entrance door.

It was unlocked.

Saxby was a fool if he thought that he was safe. Darrogh pushed through the opening and then crept into the flat. Breanon and Savis followed, moving out on each side of him. They moved forward in unison, scanning the room as they made their way to the area of the floor that was lighted.

There was the sound of a hand slapping bare skin.

Ahead, Darrogh could see two people. A man who was holding a woman by the back of her neck over the edge of a chair arm. He could not see if it were Tamsin, but the dress was the same color as the one she had been wearing this evening. There was no struggle, so the woman might be a willing participant. He could not take that chance.

Darrogh controlled his breathing.

He inched his way closer.

"Stop," he said as he placed his pistol on the man's temple.

"What the hell?" The man started to turn and Darrogh pulled back the trigger of his gun. "Do not move."

"How did you get in?"

"No lock can stop a Hunter." Darrogh's voice was cold. "Turn around slowly."

The man raised his hands and turned. He was tall for a human, but still shorter than Darrogh. He was the same man who owned the vehicle Tamsin had driven away in. He was bare-chested and the zipper was down on his pants.

The woman's dress was over her head and she made no attempt to cover herself. She did not move or speak. Darrogh pulled her dress down. It was obvious that Saxby had intended to have sex with her.

He did not know if it was consensual.

He grabbed George Saxby by the shoulder and threw him at Breanon. Breanon trained his rifle on Saxby, who backed himself up against a side table. Only when the man was under their control did Darrogh look at the woman. He knelt beside her and turned her face so he could see if it were Tamsin. It was only a formality because from the moment they had entered the flat, he had known she was there. There was a red mark across her cheek and tears running down her face. His thumb brushed the tears away. Her eyes were still filled with terror.

"Do you want us to leave?"

"Of course she does." Saxby shouted. "You idiots have ruined everything."

"Please." The word was so faint that Darrogh had to bend closer to hear. "Help."

Her words were slurred, but unmistakable.

"Kill him." Darrogh stood.

"What?" Saxby sputtered. "You can't get away with that."

Darrogh lifted Tamsin off the chair. The bodice of her dress was torn so he took his jacket off and put it around her shoulders before easing her back into the chair. She didn't resist him. Neither did she help. He frowned and looked at her eyes. They were bloodshot and she could barely keep them open.

"What did you drug her with?"

"Why should I tell you?"

"I can make your death quick and painless, or drag it out. Which would you prefer?"

"Neither." Saxby crossed his arms over his bare chest and clamped his mouth shut.

"Search the place." Darrogh ordered. "Start with the kitchen and the bottle on the counter."

Savis opened cupboards and in a few minutes he held up a bag of white pills. "It is Rohypnol."

The man had no honor. Worse, he had done harm to a woman. The Sacred Code was very clear about the consequences. George Saxby would die for what he had done to Tamsin.

"Hey, it was only a joke." Saxby's voice was a whine. "I never meant to do anything, just scare her a bit."

Darrogh looked at the video camera mounted on a tripod. "You were filming this?"

"Broadcasting." Saxby straightened his shoulders. "Everyone on the internet has seen what you've done."

"I doubt it." Savis picked the camera up and pulled the memory card from it. "The camera is not connected to a network."

"Search his flat. I want his computer and any other evidence of his activity. No one can trace this back to Tamsin."

Savis nodded and pocketed the memory card before he started searching the bookcases that lined one wall of the apartment. Darrogh flipped open the computer on his desk and searched the files. What he saw turned his stomach. Tamsin was not his first victim. There were dozens of video clips of women being abused and drugged.

This man's actions had condemned him.

"There is more here." Savis had opened a locked cupboard.

Darrogh left the computer and went to Savis. There were memory cards, video tapes and discs. All of them had labels with women's names on them. It was a neat and orderly library of George Saxby's evil.

"Make sure there is nothing with Tamsin's name on it." Darrogh turned back to Saxby. "I do not want the police making any connection with her and this monster."

Darrogh walked over to Saxby who was now standing with his hands behind his back. "You have broken every code that I live by."

"I took what they were offering." Saxby sneered. "They strut around in dresses that barely cover them. They want to entice us. All I do is give them what they're asking for."

"A crime against a woman is never tolerated."

"A good lawyer will get me off." Saxby shrugged. "You can't prove that I've done anything worse than have sex with these women."

Disgust filled Darrogh. The man showed no remorse or regret. He would never see that his actions were wrong. His abuse must stop and there was only one way to ensure that.

"I am not bound by your laws." Darrogh leaned close to Saxby. "To defile a woman is punishable by death."

Saxby's eyes widened and he took a step back, moving his arm forward as he did so.

Cold metal pressed into Darrogh's side.

The fool thought he could kill a Hunter. He was a mere human and his reflexes were too slow. Before he could pull the trigger,

Darrogh had grabbed the gun and pushed it up and away from him. It was now pointed under Saxby's head.

"Justice will be had."

Saxby struggled to push the gun away. His muscles strained with the effort and Darrogh waited until he weakened. That's when Darrogh pushed the gun higher so that it was at Saxby's temple. A second later, the gun fired.

Saxby was dead.

Darrogh let his body slump to the floor and turned away. To kill another was never pleasant, but as team leader, it was his responsibility to carry out the sentence. Having Saxby pull a gun on him had made it easier. He took a towel from the kitchen and wiped away the blood from his hands.

"Leave him for the authorities. They will probably label it a suicide." He turned to Breanon and handed him the towel. "Secure the building and make certain there is no evidence of our presence."

"Should I leave these videos here?" Savis asked. "There is nothing with Tamsin's name on it."

"Bring his computer. Leave the rest of the evidence. Saxby's victims will at least know that justice has been done."

Darrogh walked over to Tamsin. She looked to be sleeping. When he stopped beside the chair her lids fluttered opened and there was a question in her eyes. Now was not the time to tell her what had happened. Soon enough, she would learn about her attacker's fate. She needed rest and the comfort of her own bed.

He picked her up in his arms. "You are safe."

She cuddled close to his shoulder and a surge of warmth spread through him. He had never felt anything like it before. It was paralyzing and at the same time exhilarating. His heart stuttered to a stop and then started beating at a frantic pace. He was losing control over his body and he did not care.

"Thank you." Tamsin whispered. "I prayed that you would come."

Darrogh knew that he would always be there for her. She was more than a mission. He should never have held her because now he could never let her go. As much as he was connected to her, he would still have to leave after their operation was finished. It was not right for a Hunter to bond with a woman.

When they reached the door, Breanon was waiting. "I have cleaned off any surfaces that might have held prints."

"What about the lift and the cameras?"

"The camera feed went straight to his computer. The lift has been cleaned."

"Good. We will exit back through the stairs."

The weight of Tamsin in his arms gave him comfort. He had spent his life on the battlefield, mired in death and killing. This was the first time that he had been able to use his skills for saving someone. Years of training and fighting had honed the instincts that had let him reach Tamsin in time.

When they reached the bottom floor, Darrogh waited while Breanon and Savis went to clean away any evidence of Tamsin in Saxby's car. When they came back, they left by the loading door and Savis reset the keypad. No incriminating evidence would be left behind.

They kept to the shadows as they edged along the warehouse. They were almost at the street when Firbin reached out to him by mind connect.

"Tamsin's father is at her house and is insisting on seeing his daughter. What should I tell him?"

Chapter 6

Tamsin opened her eyes.

She closed them immediately.

The world was spinning and she waited a few seconds until it stopped, before looking again. This time, the bright stream of sunlight that filtered into her bedroom sent a piercing jab of pain through her skull. Her mind was fuzzy and her mouth dry. What had happened last night?

She struggled to sit upright.

That was when she remembered.

She'd gone to Beauvie's and tried in vain to lose her father's bodyguards. She'd been unsuccessful until she'd run into George Saxby. He'd agreed to give her a ride home. Glimpses of being in his apartment and talking with him, flitted through her mind. The last thing she remembered was agreeing to have a glass of wine with George.

A memory of him slapping her and ripping her dress sent a shock of horror through her.

She jumped out of bed and stumbled to her vanity mirror.

Her hand ran down the side of her face where the telltale signs of a bruise was forming. She pulled her pajama top down and saw another bruise at the base of her neck. Her hands shook and her legs could barely hold her weight.

It hadn't been a dream.

She forced herself back into bed and pulled the covers up. Questions flooded her brain. Why couldn't she remember? How did she get home? Who undressed her? Horror and dread filled Tamsin. She'd heard about women waking up and not remembering what had happened, but they'd been drugged.

"No," she whispered. "George wouldn't do that."

"He did."

The sound of Darrogh's voice sent her head flying up. He was sitting in the shadows in the corner of her bedroom. One leg was crossed over the other knee and he looked as if he'd slept in his clothes. His dark eyes were unwavering and a shiver of awareness raced up her spine.

"Why are you here?"

"Someone had to watch you. We could not risk something happening to you in your sleep." Darrogh's voice was matter of fact. "Do you remember last night?"

"Vague images and feelings." Tamsin swallowed past the lump in her throat. She dreaded the answer, but she had to ask. "Did he rape me?"

"No."

Relief flooded through her. An image of her head being pressed into the cushion and being unable to move gnawed at the back of her mind. She looked up at Darrogh. His gaze was intense and filled with concern. Another memory came rushing back. He'd looked at her like that last night after the drug had already taken effect and she was immobilized.

Darrogh had witnessed everything.

Humiliation filled her.

Her cheeks heated with embarrassment and for once, she was at a loss as to what to do. How could she ever look him in the face again? He'd seen what George had done to her. She dropped her face into her hands and groaned.

"It was not your fault."

Tamsin wanted to crawl away and hide. "I went with him."

"He was not a man to be trusted." Darrogh put both legs on the floor. "You could not have known that."

Tamsin shook her head. "I hadn't seen George in a few years. I was crazy to accept a ride from him."

"We would have taken you home."

"That was the whole point." Tamsin leaned back in her pillows. "I just wanted to go home alone. George said he'd drive me, but once I was in his car, he insisted I visit his flat."

"He had taken many women there." Darrogh's voice was matter of fact. "He will not be doing that again."

Flashes of movement and the sound of an explosion came rushing at her. Her heart hammered in her chest as she remembered the blast of a gun. Surely they hadn't killed George? The police would be all over her apartment any moment now.

"There is no need to be concerned."

"Is he alive?"

"No." Darrogh's face was impassive. He could have been announcing that dinner was being served.

"You can't murder someone in cold blood." Tamsin's voice trembled. "You'll be arrested and sent to jail."

"It was necessary. He pulled a pistol on me."

"It was self-defense." Tamsin nodded as legal strategies raced through her mind. "That means you'll probably go free."

"I would have executed him anyway. He could not live after what he did to you."

"It's wrong to take another's life." Tamsin's head was whirling with the calm manner in which Darrogh was talking about killing George.

"A Hunter lives by the Sacred Code, and metes out justice when necessary." Darrogh stood. "Your laws cannot hold me."

"The police would have arrested him."

"They will not be involved. We have taken care of everything."

"What does that mean?"

"We made certain that no one could connect you to Saxby." Darrogh flexed his shoulders.

Tamsin was transfixed by the sight.

She had never seen him in anything but a loose jacket before. Now, he was in a tight T-shirt and it emphasized his impressive physique. He looked as if he spent every waking moment in a gym. She didn't know how she'd missed that about him before. She'd been so intent on hating the men that her father had hired to spy on her, that she'd hardly noticed them.

"We do not spy."

Tamsin's breath caught in her throat. That was the second time he'd anticipated what she was thinking. "How did you guess my thoughts?"

Darrogh shrugged. "You face is easy to read. I am a trained warrior and even though I have spent little time around women, I do understand facial expressions."

"So what am I thinking now?" Tamsin crossed her arms over her chest.

Darrogh gave her a lopsided grin. "You would like some privacy. I will get your morning tea. After that, we will talk."

He left the room with a quiet click of the door.

She had to stop thinking about Darrogh. He was her bodyguard, nothing more.

Tamsin released the breath she'd been holding and pushed back her covers. Maybe she was too transparent. What she needed now was a shower, long, and hot enough to wash away George's brutal attack from last night. Nothing would truly take that away, but a shower would go a long way toward making her feel better.

When she was finished, she dressed in an old pair of ripped jeans and a loose blue blouse. She was bare of makeup and glamor this morning, and it felt good. She'd been on edge since her father had installed his henchmen in her house. She didn't care what they thought of her appearance anymore. They'd probably seen her at her worse last night. She deserved to be comfortable in her own home.

Breakfast was waiting for her in the kitchen. Tea, eggs, and toast were sitting on her glass dining table. Darrogh was also there, elbows on the tabletop and a cup of coffee in his hands. He looked comfortable. None of the other men were in sight. This was the first time since he'd been hired to guard her that they were alone together. He'd said they needed to talk and she had to agree with him. He deserved an explanation after last night, and she had some questions she wanted answered.

"I see you've been paying attention to my morning ritual." She pulled out her chair and sat.

"It is our role to attend to your needs." Darrogh watched her as she sipped her tea.

"My father only paid for you to guard me, not to be a servant."

"It is true that a Hunter usually protects and fights." Darrogh's tone was serious. "All men are meant to serve women, though."

Tamsin choked on her tea. She coughed for several seconds before she could catch her breath. Darrogh looked as if he was going to pound her back, so she raised her hand to stop him. When her breathing returned to normal she sat back and looked at him.

"You have to be kidding me."

Darrogh frowned. "Why would I do that?"

"All week you've referred to yourself as a Hunter." Tamsin shook her head. "What is a Hunter and why do men serve women?"

"A Hunter is an elite soldier that has been genetically modified to be the best warrior in the universe. We are a brotherhood and there is no force that can defeat us. We help those who ask for us."

Tamsin tilted her head. "You're mercenaries."

"We right wrongs."

"You're vigilantes then."

Tamsin rubbed her head. She was still a bit groggy after last night and Darrogh's explanation about who he was didn't help. It sounded as if science was involved, and that had never been her strong point. It only confused her. She'd let the comment about serving women pass for now.

"Are you certain my father didn't tell you why I was in danger?"

"I do not lie." Darrogh straightened his shoulders. "He did not elaborate."

Tamsin frowned. "My father has been trying to get me back under his control since I called off my wedding last year."

"I know nothing about a wedding." Darrogh took another sip of his coffee. "He requested our help. He is paying us for our security services, not to spy on you."

"Let me get this straight." Tamsin tapped the table with a finger. "You protect people without knowing where the threat is from?"

Darrogh nodded. "I was given a team and instructed to guard you."

"Who sent you here?"

"Ardal, the leader of our unit."

"And he didn't bother to find out the details?" Tamsin shook her head. "I don't believe you."

"I follow orders." Darrogh's voice was harsh. "Your father requested our help.

"I still am not convinced it's necessary for your team to be here."

Darrogh's eyes narrowed. "You needed help last night."

"And I am grateful that you came to my rescue." Tamsin's voice shook. "I just don't understand how you found me so quickly."

"A warrior needs the skills to hunt people. Your planet may have different technology, but some things are the same."

Tamsin raised her hand to stop him from speaking. He'd said planet, but he must have meant country. She knew that her father had hired these men from North America. Their accents were definitely not British. Still, he kept referring to himself as a warrior and that was a term that had gone out of favor in the middle ages. Her head hurt too much to try and figure out his meaning.

"You tracked me." Tamsin took a bite of toast. "I get that. What I want to know is how you can be so certain the police won't find me. We all leave evidence on a camera somewhere."

"We erased it."

"Are you certain you got everything?"

"We wiped the feed from Beauvie's, the streets you passed through, Saxby's apartment, and we took the memory card from his video camera."

"That's pretty thorough." Tamsin didn't hide her approval.

"None of that would have been necessary if you'd allowed us to stay with you last night." There was no anger or recrimination in Darrogh's voice. "We almost did not find you in time."

"And you think I'm ungrateful." Tamsin grimaced. She was grilling him about his methods and instead she should be thanking him. "Believe me, when I realized that George had drugged my wine, I wished I hadn't given you guys the slip."

"What did you slip?" Darrogh frowned.

"It's a saying. I should never have left the club without you."

Darrogh nodded. "We are in agreement."

Tamsin smiled and took another bite of toast. In the end it didn't really matter why her father had felt the need to hire these men. They'd saved her life and she was thankful for that. They'd also kept her name out of the whole incident and that was a miracle. The last thing she needed was more negative press. The fallout from her cancelled wedding had been bad enough. To be caught in a murder investigation would have been a nightmare.

Tamsin finished her breakfast and pushed her plate away.

"Where are the rest of your men?"

"They are waiting for us to finish our discussion." Darrogh leaned back in his chair.

"There's more?"

"It is necessary to know if you are unhappy with my command."

That was the last question Tamsin had expected. "How can you think that?"

"There is no other reason for your refusal to accept our protection and because of that, I failed to keep you safe."

Tamsin shook her head. "You don't understand."

"Explain."

She clasped her hands and took a deep breath. "You make me nervous."

"So it is my command you do not trust." Darrogh's eyes narrowed. "I will request another team leader for you."

"No." Tamsin reached out and touched his arm. A jolt of sensation raced up her fingers and when she looked up at Darrogh, his expression was grim. "You felt that too."

He nodded. "It is best that I leave you."

"I don't want anyone else." Tamsin's voice was low.

"I cannot provide protection if you continue to fight me."

"If I understood the reason for you being here, it might be easier." Tamsin stood and picked up her plate. "You can't ask me to blindly believe that I'm in danger."

"There was no doubt of it last night."

Tamsin put her plate in the sink and looked back at Darrogh. "I wouldn't have been in that situation if I'd been on my own. I don't enjoy going to clubs like Beauvie's."

"Why go?" Darrogh stood.

"To bug you guys enough so that you'd leave me alone." Tamsin's voice rose in exasperation. "I didn't want bodyguards."

"Then we will leave. No other team will replace us." Darrogh walked to the counter with his empty mug.

"As easy as that?"

"Yes." Darrogh put his cup in the sink. "There are many who desire our help. We do not need to stay where we are not wanted."

Pain shot through Tamsin at the thought of being left alone. It was ridiculous because Darrogh was offering to give her what she'd been asking for all week. Now that she had it, her victory felt hollow. She couldn't explain why, but the thought of being parted from Darrogh was unbearable.

"Great." Her voice was low. "When will you go?"

"Immediately." Darrogh hesitated a second. "It is best this way. It has been difficult this past week."

Tamsin rolled her eyes. At least she wasn't the only one who'd found it challenging. "Next time you guard a woman, you should make certain she wants you in her house."

"I will suggest it."

Darrogh looked down at her with an intent gaze. Her breath caught in her throat and for a second, she thought he was going to kiss her. Instead, he backed away.

"I will tell the men that we are to leave."

"Can you thank them for me?" Tamsin squeezed her hands together. "You all saved my life last night. George intended to kill me."

"It is even better that he is dead." Darrogh nodded and turned.

At that moment, Firbin entered the kitchen. "Tamsin's father is insisting that we bring her to his house. He has received another threat."

"Does my father know about last night?"

Firbin shook his head. "He came to your house and wanted to see you. I told him you were asleep."

Tamsin frowned. "Do you think he heard about Saxby and that is the threat he is referring to?"

"I do not know." Darrogh's tone was neutral.

Tamsin bit her lip. Suddenly the thought of facing her father alone was more than she could handle. If there was a threat against her, then it would be best if she waited before sending the men away. What harm would a couple more hours of protection do?

"Could you stay with me until I find out what my father is concerned about?"

"As you wish." Darrogh took her elbow and led her out of the kitchen. "We will take you to Sir Robert's house."

"Do you believe him?" Tamsin grabbed her jacket and purse from the closet.

"Things may be different now." Darrogh looked down at her. "You will have to ask your father to be honest with you. That is the only way you can make a decision about whether we need to continue protecting you."

Darrogh shut the door of the house behind her. The rest of the unit were waiting for them. The van and Tamsin's vehicle were parked at the curb. She felt a moment of embarrassment until Savis nodded at her. She smiled and the men gathered so that she was the center of their protective shield. During the past week, it had felt ridiculous to go out on the street like this, but not today.

She felt safe.

Darrogh was by her side and that gave her courage. She needed to know why her father was worried and she was determined to get answers.

Chapter 7

Darrogh's eyes narrowed as he entered the study with Tamsin.

Savis and Kerm, were behind them. Breanon had set up surveillance on the grounds and Firbin and Jehon were with the vehicles. Darrogh had ordered full protection protocol after last night and everyone was on alert. He was not going to allow anything to happen to Tamsin again.

There was an understated elegance about Sir Robert Creighton's house. Painted in warm earth tones and filled with plush carpets, antiques, and leather furniture, it was a stark contrast to the metal and glass fixtures of Tamsin's modern townhouse.

He guided Tamsin to a leather couch and waited until she was comfortable before turning his attention to her father. Sir Robert was seated behind a large mahogany desk. At sixty-three, he was still in control of the family bank that he'd inherited in his twenties. Creighton's was one of the oldest and most respected private banks in England. It did business with the very rich and powerful. Sir Robert Creighton understood what it took to command. He was a man used to being obeyed.

His assistant Henry Kingsley, was standing beside him.

Kingsley was almost forty years old, with auburn hair and a short-cropped beard. Darrogh had read the file on him before arriving in London. Ardal, had requested the records of all of the employees of Creighton's Bank that Tamsin might have had contact with before they had agreed to guard her. Kingsley had worked as Sir Robert's personal assistant for the past fifteen years and was trusted without question.

Darrogh looked around the luxurious study, noting the large windows and bright sunlight shining in. It would be easy for a gunman to target anyone inside. He looked back at their host.

"Close the drapes."

After a few seconds of silence, Creighton nodded to his assistant to do as Darrogh had requested. Once the room had been darkened and privacy was assured, Darrogh turned to Sir Robert.

"Tell us why you have insisted on this meeting."

"I've received another threat."

"I must know the details."

"I can't tell you." Creighton pursed his lips.

"It is impossible for us to continue defending her like this."

Darrogh's tone was harsh. Tamsin had almost been killed last night because this man had refused to tell her the truth. Darrogh was bred and trained to obey orders and succeed. If he was going to continue keeping Tamsin safe, he needed all the information.

"They insisted that I stay quiet." Sir Robert shook his head. "These people will kill Tamsin if I don't do what they ask."

"You can't expect me to just accept your word for it, Dad." Tamsin raised her voice from where she was seated. Darrogh sensed her agitation and sent her a wave of calm. They needed to convince her father to help, not antagonize him.

"You have to trust me on this." Robert Creighton ran his hand though his graying hair.

"You've had me guarded for a week now and there has been no threat."

"These people are too clever to show themselves, but they'll know if I don't obey." Sir Robert's voice was tense. "You can't fool them."

"Who are they?" Darrogh's voice was sharp.

Robert Creighton shrugged. "I've never met them."

"You're just using this as an excuse to have me followed," Tamsin insisted. "You've been trying to control my life since Mum died when I was ten."

"That's not true." Creighton pounded his fist on his desk. "I have protected you and have always done what was best."

"Like marrying Winchester Nethercott." Tamsin's voice was filled with scorn.

"We needed the merger with his bank."

Tamsin shook her head. "I let you talk me into marrying that snake, yet there is only so much a woman can stand. I'm just thankful I found out about him before it was too late."

"I know he wasn't perfect." Robert Creighton's tone was conciliatory.

Tamsin gave a short laugh. "He couldn't even wait until the wedding before he started cheating on me."

"We needed the merger to protect ourselves and marrying him was the best solution. Thanks to your refusal, we're running out of options."

Tamsin's eyes widened. "You think I should have married him even though I caught him in bed with my best friend, Liz."

Robert Creighton smoothed a hand down his tie. "That was unfortunate."

"A broken dish is unfortunate." Tamsin's tone was sarcastic.

"Nethercott has no honor." Darrogh interrupted the argument. He needed more information about the threats "Why did you need the merger? Is the bank in trouble financially?"

A muscle tightened in Sir Robert's jaw. He glanced up at Henry, who shrugged. It took a few more seconds of silence before Sir Robert nodded and turned back to Darrogh.

"A group of men visited me about a year ago and insisted that they have access to my bank's clients." Robert Creighton sat back in his leather desk chair. "I thought they were joking. I was wrong. They suggested that I form a partnership with Nethercott's to make it easier for the takeover of both our banks. They gave me a year to make the arrangements."

Darrogh frowned. To threaten two long established banks in a stable country was a bold move. He had been on Earth long enough to know that banks were the financial heart of this planet. Everything depended on them, from personal savings to the economy of countries.

"Did they tell you who they were?"

"The Albirsion Corporation." Creighton pulled a file folder out of his desk drawer and threw it at Darrogh. "I'm not a fool. I looked into the organization and was astonished by what I found. They are involved in everything from mining, real estate, communications, and banks."

Darrogh's internal defense mechanism went to high alert when he heard the name. It was too close to Albireon to be a coincidence. Albireons were a race of aliens who had somehow insinuated themselves into one of the major military installations in Australia. Now it seemed as if their influence was greater than he, and the other Hunters, suspected.

From the list of their companies and holdings that Sir Robert's investigation had uncovered, it looked as if they had enough control of the planet's resources and finances to set up a shadow government. If that was the case, it would not be long before they would conquer Earth and wipe out the humans.

Invading planets was what they did. First they would harvest all of the genetic material from the populace. At a later date they could recombine it with other genes and create new slave species to sell. Annihilating a species gave them exclusive control over the planet's genome in the universal genetic market. It was only a matter of time before they carried this out on Earth.

Albireons were the scourge of the universe.

"Did you do what they asked?" Darrogh kept his gaze trained on Robert Creighton.

"No." Sir Robert shook his head. "Creighton's has built its reputation on discretion. Our clients are some of the richest people in the world and they look to us to keep their finances and identities private. All that would be destroyed if this Albirsion Corporation took over the bank."

"Then why did you want me to marry Nethercott?" Tamsin's voice cracked.

"I thought that if I pretended to want the merger it would buy me time. Once the banks were amalgamated, then together, we'd be able to stop these people. We'd be stronger and less vulnerable to a takeover."

"So you were willing to sacrifice me." Tamsin's voice was filled with pain.

"It wasn't like that." Her father's tone was pleading. "You liked Winchester and I thought he'd take good care of you."

"I don't need a man to watch over me." Tamsin straightened her shoulders. "You should have told me what was going on. I was working at the bank. I deserved to know."

"I wanted to protect you." Her father exhaled. "You don't know these people. They kept coming back with bigger threats and when the wedding was called off they said they'd kill you if their orders weren't followed."

"When was the first direct threat on Tamsin's life?" Darrogh closed the file folder he'd been looking through.

"About a month before I contacted you people." Sir Robert leaned forward in his chair. "I had several private agencies watching Tamsin, but they kept losing her. I needed someone who wouldn't fail. That's when I found your website."

"What site?" Tamsin's eyes widened.

"AHunter4Hire.com," Darrogh answered. "That is how people employ our services."

"Your site stated that you could help when no one else would." Sir Robert shrugged. "I said that my daughter's life was being threatened and I was willing to pay. I didn't lie."

"You should have told us the complete truth. You have wasted valuable time." Darrogh turned around and motioned to Savis. He handed him the file folder with the list of Albirsion companies. "Contact Ardal and let him know that we are probably dealing with Albireons."

"You've heard of them?" Creighton's assistant Henry spoke for the first time.

Darrogh nodded. "We are familiar with them."

"They sound like bullies," Tamsin said. "You can't possibly take their threats seriously."

"They sent me another message yesterday. It was very explicit." Sir Robert nodded to his assistant Henry. "Show them the note."

Henry pulled a sheet of paper from his jacket and handed it to Darrogh. It was written on thick vellum by someone who was skilled at calligraphy. The message was short and to the point.

We will kill your daughter on Saturday if you do not hand over the bank.

Saturday was three days away.

Darrogh passed the note to Tamsin.

"Can you protect her?" Creighton's voice shook. "I need to know."

"Yes, now that we know who we are fighting." Darrogh's voice was definite. "I have fought the Albireons many times and been successful. It will not be easy. Your daughter needs to depart London. There is no way to protect her here."

"I'm not leaving my home." Tamsin's protest echoed through the room. "I refuse to run away."

Darrogh held back his objection. She was a woman and should be obeyed. If she insisted, then they would protect her in London. There was still the problem of the Albireons and their demands. The information in Sir Robert's file suggested that the Albireons had far-reaching tentacles on this planet. It would be difficult to hide from them.

"Can you negotiate an extension on their deadline?"

"What do you think I've been doing for the past year?" Creighton clenched his hand into a fist. "They refuse to give me anymore time."

Creighton's assistant Henry Kinsley cleared his throat. "I have advised Sir Robert to at least let them into the bank. One of the people from Albirsion Corporation could sit on the Board."

"They will not stop there." Darrogh's voice was definite. "Do you know how many more banks they have taken over?"

Henry pulled a small booklet from his pocket and flipped through the pages. "They have controlling interests in fifty banks across the world."

"You can't let them have Creighton's." Tamsin's tone was forceful. "Even if they kill me."

Creighton's face paled. "I can't lose you."

"It will not come to that." Darrogh's voice was hard. "We have accepted the mission of protecting you. A Hunter does not fail."

"Thank you." Creighton wiped a hand across his face. "I know I should give them the bank. It's only a business, but my family has owned it since the sixteenth century. It has been handed down from one generation to the next and I intend to pass it on to Tamsin intact."

"We need to ensure that the bank is protected." Darrogh looked over to Savis.

"Ardal agrees. Creighton's Bank must not be lost to the Albireons."

Tamsin frowned. "I didn't realize you'd left the room. How do you propose to keep the bank safe?"

"Ardal is sending more men." Savis spoke in a matter of fact voice. "With your Father's help, we will be able to shut down the takeover."

"Once they realize that we are shielding the bank, they will know that they are the ones that are vulnerable," Darrogh explained.

"I don't understand." Sir Robert's voice was filled with confusion. "You protect people. How can you stop a business takeover?"

"We are skilled in many things." Darrogh's voice was dry. "They will hesitate to continue their threats once they realize that they are dealing with Hunters."

"They don't scare easily." Sir Robert stood. "I have been trying to get control of this situation for the past year. The best solution I had was to merge our bank with Nethercott's so that we'd be stronger together, and able to fight the takeover this corporation was pushing for."

"We understand how they work." Darrogh glanced at Henry. "Do you have any contact information for this organization?"

Henry ripped a page from his notebook. "This is all I have."

Darrogh glanced down at the sheet. There were a couple of names and telephone numbers and one email address. It was a start. He handed the sheet to Savis.

"Give this information to Ardal."

He went over to Tamsin "It is time we left."

She nodded and stood. "Give me a few minutes alone with my father."

"We will wait outside the room."

He motioned for the rest of the team to leave. Henry followed them out too. When the door was closed behind them Darrogh sent Kerm to guard the entryway. Now all he had to do was convince Tamsin that staying in London was not the best option.

Henry cleared his throat. "Do you really think you can stop this organization?"

"They have gained much control, but we are familiar with their tactics. It is not the first time we have battled Albireons."

"You keep talking about them as if they're a race or citizens of another country." Henry gave a short laugh. "This is business, pure and simple."

Darrogh considered the man for a few seconds and then shook his head. "It is about world domination."

Henry crossed his arms. "It's simple economics."

"If the Albireons gain control of this planet's resources and industries, it means the decimation of the human species."

"That's nuts." Henry shook his head. "You guys are crazy. I'm not certain where Mr. Creighton found you, but I doubt you'll be able to stop anyone from hurting his daughter. Don't think I'm not going to tell him about this conversation."

"Just because you do not believe in the threat does not make it less real."

Darrogh turned away from the assistant. It was a waste of his time to convince this man. The Albireons were on earth and if they had power over so much of this planet's assets and institutions, then their threat was greater than they had guessed.

The study door opened and Tamsin came out. "I'm ready to go home."

Darrogh started for the entrance. "Wait until the car arrives."

Jehon pulled up a few seconds later. Darrogh stood beside Tamsin, covering her body with his, until she was in the vehicle. Then he signaled the rest of his team. They would follow in the van and keep the car in sight at all times. Darrogh sat beside Tamsin and shut the door.

"Do you believe that my father has any chance of holding off this corporate takeover?"

Darrogh glanced over at Tamsin. "They will succeed unless he has something to threaten them with."

"So he might as well hand the bank over now?" There was disbelief in Tamsin's voice.

"That is not what I said." Darrogh kept his tone neutral. "We will find a way to stop them, but it will take time. Until we have a solution, you need to let us protect you."

"By taking me out of London?"

"Yes."

"This is my home. I refuse to leave it."

She was being illogical. Darrogh knew that he should obey her wishes because she was a woman. This situation was different. He had to do what was best for her security. Now was not the time to insist she leave the city, though. He would try and convince her of that once they were safely at her home.

"You told my father you could protect me."

"Not this way." Darrogh turned in the seat to look at her. "You cannot expect me to continue guarding you without your cooperation."

Just then, there was a loud noise and the car jerked to the side. Darrogh threw himself over Tamsin. Jehon was fighting to gain control of the vehicle as it skidded across the road and over the sidewalk.

They came to a stop just before crashing into a pole.

When he looked down there was blood on his hands.

Tamsin was injured.

Chapter 8

"I can't breathe." Tamsin tried to push Darrogh away.

"Be still." His voice was a low whisper as he shifted his weight off her. "We must be certain it is safe."

"It was a tire blowout, that's all."

"Jehon is very thorough about checking the vehicle."

She could feel the tension in Darrogh's body.

"The tires were fine."

Darrogh wasn't going to let her up until he was ready. She took a deep breath and relaxed. She felt safe with him and even though it was probably just a freak accident, she'd let him play the hero.

A vehicle stopped beside them. The door opened and she could hear footsteps running toward them. Could Darrogh have been right about them being followed? It was crazy to think that someone could be attacked in broad daylight in a city as busy as London. Surely someone would stop them?

"There is no need for concern. It is my men." Darrogh eased himself away from her. "You are bleeding."

Tamsin brushed her fingers across her forehead. It was sticky and wet. "I must have hit my head when the car lurched forward."

Darrogh turned her so that she faced him. He moved her hair away and examined the cut. "It is minor. It has almost stopped bleeding."

Tamsin leaned back against the seat. "What do we do now?"

"Once the area is secured, we will move you to the van and continue to your house."

It took a few minutes before she was hurried into the rear of the van. Darrogh used his body to shield her, and only left her side once she was safely inside the vehicle. Firbin was in the driver's seat. Breanon sat with his rifle aimed out the tinted window on one side of the van, while Kerm did the same on the opposite. A shiver went through her. These men didn't think this had been an accident.

When had her life become so dangerous? All she wanted was to go home and relax. To put her feet up on the couch and forget about the ordeals she'd been through in the last twenty-four hours.

The van door opened and Darrogh and Savis jumped in before slamming the rear door closed. Darrogh sat beside her while Savis went to a computer that was mounted on a shelf behind the driver's seat. Neither man looked at her or spoke. As if on silent command, both Kerm and Breanon seemed to tense and tighten their hold on their weapons.

The vehicle jerked forward.

"Is everything all right?"

"There was a bullet in the tire." Darrogh's voice was matter of fact. "It was meant as a warning."

Tamsin's heart started to beat at a furious rate. "How can you be certain?"

"We would be dead otherwise. They need you alive until your father submits to their demands." Darrogh's tone was dry. "We have to get you to safety."

"If I start running, I'll never stop." Tamsin pushed away her fear. "You can't submit to people like this."

"Protecting yourself so that you can fight another day is not giving in. Retreat is an honorable and often successful strategy." Darrogh's voice remained calm. "These people will not stop until they have carried out their threat. They have no concern for human life and they consider you disposable."

"We should go to the police and tell them." Tamsin clasped her hands together to prevent them from shaking. She had never seen Darrogh so serious before and it scared her. "If they're as bad as you say, then they shouldn't be walking around free."

Darrogh's jaw clenched. "They do not answer to anyone."

"That's ridiculous." Tamsin muttered. "Everyone has to be accountable or there would be chaos."

"Exactly." Darrogh gave her an intense stare.

His eyes were cold with determination and knowledge.

A shiver of fear raced up her spine.

What wasn't he telling her? She needed answers. First, her father tells her that some organization is demanding he hand over his bank or she'll be killed. Then Darrogh is insisting that there is no way to combat these people.

"I didn't say that." Darrogh leaned close to her. "We can fight, but not in London."

Tamsin's eyes narrowed. "You read my thoughts again."

Darrogh nodded. "We will talk about this once you are safe."

Tamsin crossed her arms and leaned back against the side panel of the van. "I intend to know about everything that is happening."

"As you wish."

There was silence until they reached her house. The van pulled up to the curb and everyone except Firbin, jumped out and surrounded her. If she hadn't just been shot at, she would have thought it was ridiculous. When she had the answers to her questions, then she would decide what needed to be done.

Darrogh used her key to unlock her door and then waited with her outside until the rest of the team had cleared the apartment. Only then, was she allowed to enter her home.

"Are there any listening devices?"

"None." Savis stated in a matter of fact tone. "Ardal has been informed of the current situation. He will be in contact with further instructions."

Darrogh nodded and then turned to her. "You may relax now."

"I'm going to lock myself in my bedroom and take a nap." Tamsin turned to Darrogh and poked her finger into his chest. "After that, you and I are going to have a serious discussion."

A fission of heat raced up her arm.

The breath caught in her throat.

She'd never experienced attraction like this before. It was raw and primal. She fought the urge to fling herself into his arms and beg him to hold her forever. As soon as the thought had crossed her mind, she was appalled with herself. He was her bodyguard. She might trust him with her life, but never with her heart.

She swallowed and backed away.

Darrogh's gaze never left her face. She could have sworn she'd felt his thoughts brush across her mind. A calm acceptance of what had just passed between them. It was impossible. It had to be her imagination brought on by her throbbing headache, and the aftereffects of the drug that Saxby had given her. There was no other explanation.

"You should rest." Darrogh's voice was hoarse.

Tamsin nodded and turned to go to her room when the phone rang.

She sighed and picked up the receiver. "Hello."

"Tamsin, we need to talk."

It was Winchester Nethercott.

Darrogh looked at her and she shook her head. After everything that had happened in the last day, she couldn't face her ex-fiancé right now. The truth was that there would never be a good time to face him.

"We have nothing to discuss." Tamsin went to hang the phone up when Winchester's voice stopped her.

"Your father told me everything that is happening. I can help."

Tamsin hesitated.

She didn't trust Winchester, but she couldn't afford to refuse help right now. Men were threatening her father's bank and her life. If Winchester had a way to deal with this threat, then she needed to listen to him.

"How?"

"I can't discuss it over the phone. Meet me at the Café Organic on Kensington High Street. I'll tell you then."

Tamsin was familiar with the café. It was a risk leaving the house, yet could she pass up the chance that Winchester might be able to help? She couldn't bear to see her father upset anymore over her safety. If she could stop this crazy takeover and threats, then she had to try.

She glanced down at her watch. "I'll meet you there in one hour."

"Great. You won't regret it." Winchester hung up.

"Where are you going?"

"My ex-fiancé says that he has a way to help me." Tamsin put the receiver down. "He wants to meet me."

Darrogh shook his head. "We need to guard you and the best place to do that is here."

"I have to see him." Tamsin's voice rose. "I need to hear what he has to say. He and my father might have hatched this plan about threatening letters and corporate takeovers between them. All of it might be nonsense."

"The bullet was real." Darrogh's voice was solemn.

"It might not have been for me." Tamsin shook off her feeling of dread. "If Winchester can help, then I want to meet with him."

Darrogh frowned. It was several seconds before he answered. "We will go with you."

"You can stay outside the café while I talk to Winchester."

"No." Darrogh crossed his arms. "Your protection is my responsibility. Either I sit with you or you will stay here."

Tamsin thought about arguing, but it would be senseless. Darrogh wasn't going to relent. She bit her lower lip and considered her options. She could lose them along the way. She glanced up to see Darrogh staring at her with an intense expression on his face. A shiver went down her spine. She didn't know how he did it, but he knew what she was thinking.

Heat flooded her cheeks as shame and chagrin filled her. She'd almost died last night because she'd tried to escape their protection. She was lucky that they'd found her before she'd been injured. She refused to believe that there were threats on her life. She couldn't ignore it though.

"You can come."

"A wise decision."

"You would have followed me anyway." Tamsin rolled her eyes. "I'm not a fool. I know I took a crazy risk last night. Is it so wrong to want privacy and independence?"

"You will have that once we have taken care of the Albirsion Corporation."

Tamsin sighed. "Corporations like Albirsion run the world. There is very little that can be done about them."

"You would give up?"

"I think we should be realistic about what we can accomplish. Some things are bigger than us."

"A Hunter does not stop until he has succeeded." Darrogh turned to go into the lounge. "I will advise the team of your excursion."

Thirty minutes later, Tamsin found herself sitting in the rear of the van. Her car had been repaired and was following them. They stopped in front of the Café Organic. Breanon and Kerm left the vehicle first. Darrogh waited with her for several minutes before helping her out.

"Was that necessary?" Tamsin didn't hide her irritation. The cloak and dagger stuff was making her tense.

"The men are in position and can provide protection in case something goes wrong."

"Winchester might be a poor excuse for a human being, but he isn't stupid." Tamsin's tone was dry. "If he's been talking with my father, he knows that I have protection."

"Most humans underestimate a Hunter's abilities."

Darrogh's expression was impassive and Tamsin shook her head. He kept referring to Earth and humans as if he were separate from it. She wanted to ask him to explain, but this wasn't the time. She spotted Winchester across the small café. Blonde with grey eyes, he used his good looks and charm to get what he wanted and it looked as if he intended to do the same today. He was waiting beside a table, a chair pulled out and a wide grin on his handsome face.

Winchester Nethercott stood there as if he expected her to welcome him with open arms. He had betrayed her a week before their wedding in the worse possible way. She'd sworn never to speak to him again, and yet here she was meeting him at a café to discuss options. She was the one who should have her head examined.

He winked at her. "You took your time."

He bent to hug her. Darrogh put his hand out and stopped him.

Winchester frowned. "Who the hell are you?"

Darrogh pushed Winchester back a couple of steps. "You can speak with Tamsin from a distance and you may not touch her. If you cannot follow the rules, we leave."

"Is this the new boyfriend?"

"No." Tamsin and Darrogh answered at the same time.

"Obviously a sore point." Winchester shrugged and plopped down on the metal chair. "I need to speak to you in private."

"I stay."

Darrogh pulled out a chair for her and waited until she was seated before sitting himself. He crossed his arms and leaned back from the table. He was a forbidding sight and his message was clear. He was not going to let Winchester get away with anything. Tamsin felt the tension leave her body. With Darrogh and the rest of his team close, she had nothing to fear. Winchester was a liar and a cheat, but he had never physically threatened her before. It was comforting to know that she was protected if he tried anything.

"Tell me what you have to say." Tamsin bit the words out. "I don't want to be here longer than necessary."

"Still sore about Liz?" Winchester shrugged. "It was just a hook up. It didn't mean anything. Besides, you and I weren't legally wed yet."

"What is a hook up?" Darrogh asked.

Tamsin's cheeks heated. "I found them in bed together."

Darrogh's expression hardened. "He has no honor."

"Nobody asked your opinion." Winchester shifted his position on the chair, the metal squeaking with each move. "I'd prefer you to leave so I can talk to Tamsin."

"I will not leave her alone with a dishonest man."

Darrogh leaned closer. His presence was menacing and Tamsin had to stop herself from laughing at the expression on Winchester's face. For the first time in his life, someone was standing up to him. His charm and looks were not going to help him.

Winchester hesitated a second and then looked at her. "Your father has told me about the threats he's been receiving. I think we should go ahead with the marriage."

"I know you don't care about my safety, so what is this really about?"

"It's a good business move." Winchester lowered his voice. "I miss you."

"You think that if you marry me and I die, you'll get everything." Tamsin's voice hardened. "Do you take me for a fool?"

"I know you're still angry, but I'm trying to help." Winchester sounded sincere. "Your father thinks that if we merge the banks we'll be strong enough to prevent a takeover."

"There's no guarantee that will stop the bank from being seized."

"I could protect you." Winchester's voice took on a coaxing tone. "Together we can fight these people."

"You are not equipped to fight them." Darrogh's voice interrupted. "You cannot help."

"That's not true." Winchester paused for a second. "They've contacted me. They've assured me that if we marry, they will leave you alone."

Tamsin blinked. "Why would they care if we were married or not?"

Winchester shrugged. "They like the idea of the banks being one. It fits in with their plans I suppose."

"What plans?" Tamsin asked.

"They have a vision of a global community where every person on the planet would have a decent life." Winchester's voice was full of enthusiasm. "I know how interested you are in solutions for the Third World's economic freedom. Now's your chance to get on board with a group that can make that happen."

"Why the sudden interest in those less fortunate?" Tamsin's defenses were triggered. "You always thought my plan for creating banks in the poorer countries was crazy."

"I've changed. "Winchester cleared his throat. "Since losing you, I've realized what's important in life."

"You lie." Darrogh's harsh tone broke the spell that Winchester was weaving. For a second Tamsin had almost believed him. "What is the real reason?"

Winchester started to speak, but stopped when the waitress came to their table. They all ordered coffee and once the woman left, Tamsin turned back to Winchester.

"You were about to tell us the truth."

"Ouch." Winchester grinned. "You haven't loss your sharp tongue."

"I'm waiting."

Winchester lowered his voice. "This is our opportunity to get in on the ground floor of something big. We'll be rich if we tie our future to these people."

"You will be dead if you do."

Chapter 9

Darrogh's words were met by silence.

Winchester shook his head. "What do you know about these people? You look like you've never left a gym long enough to see the sunshine."

"I know from experience."

The waitress came with their coffees.

Darrogh was glad that Tamsin had not dismissed his words as quickly as her ex-fiancé. The man was a fool. She was lucky to have escaped marrying him. It had taken all of his training to stop from throttling Winchester when he had admitted to betraying her in such a casual way.

If a Hunter bonded, it was with only one mate. Even death could not break the bond. Darrogh had scoffed at the idea of such a pair bond even though he had seen some of his unit find mates on this planet. He had refused to believe.

Meeting Tamsin had changed that.

He was connected to her.

He was seldom in the presence of women and now he was with Tamsin all the time. That was the only reasonable explanation for how he felt. To accept that Hunters could pair bond was not an option. Having a mate was forbidden for a Hunter and he still lived by the code that had kept him alive on Cygnus. The best thing he could do was find out who was targeting Tamsin, kill them, and then leave.

"What experience?" Tamsin asked as soon as the waitress left.

"This organization is run by the Albireons. They are a race that will harvest everything they need from a planet and then destroy it."

Winchester's mouth dropped open. "Where did you get this guy?"

"My father hired him."

Winchester shook his head. "These people are businessmen. They only care about a profit."

"That is true."

Darrogh could not deny that the Albireons sought revenue. Their business was harvesting the resources and genes from planets so that they could create recombinant species that they could sell as slaves. That was where the real income was in the universal genetic market.

"They wish to use your genes." Darrogh chose his words carefully. Most humans were unaware that there were non-terrestrial species on Earth.

"They're interested in genetics?" Tamsin's voice was doubtful.

"They collect different species' genomes."

"And that includes humans."

Darrogh nodded. "Once they have all that they need, they will take over everything and destroy you."

"Wow." Winchester chuckled. "You should write fiction."

"Why would you think this?" There was a slight tremor in Tamsin's voice. "Everything points to this being a simple corporate takeover bid."

"That does not explain the threat on your life." Darrogh could see the wariness in Tamsin's eyes and decided to go for the logical approach. "Do corporations threaten to kill if they do not get the businesses they want?"

"Not legitimate ones." Tamsin frowned. "That makes Albirsion Corporation illegal and corrupt, not killers seeking world domination."

"I don't care if they want to control the whole world." Winchester announced. "This is our chance to get in on the ground floor. These guys are offering us the opportunity to control the world's banking operations."

Tamsin looked down at her coffee. "That sounds as if you've been in negotiations with them."

"There's nothing wrong in listening." Winchester shrugged. "Once we're married and our banks are merged, then the world is open to anything we want."

Darrogh held his breath as he waited for Tamsin's answer. He shouldn't care if she chose to marry this man, but he did.

"I don't want to marry you." Tamsin looked up. "I don't care about controlling the world's banks or working with this corporation."

"They will take your father's bank whether he agrees or not." Winchester tapped his forefinger on the table. "This way you'll have a say over what they do with the assets."

"You sound very certain of this." Darrogh was not fooled by the smooth talk of this man. He was hiding something and he wanted to know what. "When did you speak with these people?"

"I had a meeting a couple of days ago." Winchester turned his back on Darrogh. "Look Tami, this is between you and me."

"Don't call me that." Tamsin straightened her back. "I didn't like that nickname even when we were a couple."

Winchester held his hands up in a conciliatory motion. "No problem. We need to say yes to these guys and get things rolling. The sooner the merger takes place, the sooner we'll start raking in the bonuses."

"Is money all that is important to you?"

Winchester's eyes widened. "Of course. It should be important to you also. Money is the commodity that banks deal with."

"That doesn't mean it has to rule your life." Tamsin shook her head. "Money is a tool, nothing more. It's what you do with it that matters."

"You mean spend it."

"I mean use it for good."

Winchester shook his head. "You need to help yourself first. This is your opportunity to get in front of this before your family's bank is taken out."

"I won't let that happen."

"There's no stopping it." Winchester's voice was bitter. "Trust me. The sooner you accept these guys, the better."

"It sounds as if you already have." Darrogh could tell from Winchester's expression that he was right. "How long has your family bank been in their control?"

"Two years now."

Tamsin gasped. "Why didn't you tell me sooner?"

"What difference did it make? As long as we married and the banks were merged there was no need for you to know."

"You never intended to tell me about the threat to my father's bank."

"No." Winchester's voice was harsh. "I would have been in control of everything. Neither you nor your father would have known the difference. You could go on with your idealistic daydreams, and your father would have retired. Instead, you called the whole thing off."

"I caught you in bed with my best friend."

"Liz was hardly your friend." Winchester scoffed. "You didn't seem too interested in that aspect of our lives anyway. A man has needs and if his fiancée is unwilling to fulfill them, then he will look elsewhere."

"So now it's my fault that you cheated?" Tamsin's voice was full of disgust.

"Yes." Winchester threw himself back in his chair. "You've been given a second chance to make this right. Take their offer. You've been warned. They will kill you."

"The penalty for threatening the life of a woman is death." Darrogh pushed his chair away from the table. "A man that would carry the threat of another is either a coward or a monster."

"I'm being realistic." Winchester's voice had lost its charm."

"You've already sold out." Tamsin's tone was filled with disgust. "How could you?"

"It's called survival," Winchester hissed. "You should try it."

"Your family's bank is almost as old as ours. What about your obligation to your clients?"

"I can't help them if I'm dead." Winchester raised an eyebrow. "You should consider their offer. You could negotiate start-ups for your charity banks."

A feeling of unease crawled up Darrogh's back.

Danger was near.

He looked around the café. Nothing had changed. Firbin was still sitting at the table beside them, his hands hidden in his jacket to conceal his weapon. Jehon sat at the door, guarding the entrance. Kerm was in Tamsin's car, ready to drive them if something happened. Savis was in the communications van parked in a side street where he could keep an eye on the building. Breanon was on the roof of the next building, guarding rear and side entrances.

"*Report.*" Darrogh's command by mind connect was sharp.

"*No activity,*" Breanon said. "*No one has entered or left from the rear or side.*"

"*Two men dressed in long black coats have walked past the café twice.*" Savis's voice was tense. "*Permission to intervene.*"

"*Stay at your post. Jehon will pursue.*" Darrogh looked behind at Jehon and nodded. Jehon stood and left the café. He went outside and leaned against the building. If the men passed again, he would follow.

Darrogh still had a sense of unease. "*Firbin be prepared to move.*"

"This will be the last time they negotiate with you." Winchester was still trying to convince Tamsin to join the Albirsion group. "These are very powerful people."

Tamsin shook her head. "All the more reason to say no."

"You're a fool." Winchester stood and threw some bills on the table. "I should have saved my breath."

"I can't sell out the bank or my father."

Winchester gave a short laugh. "I convinced the group to let me give you another chance because I felt I owed it to you. We're even now."

"There is no forgetting what you did." Tamsin shook her head. "Do you really think threatening me would make your betrayal go away?"

Winchester leaned over the table. "They're going to kill you. What will happen to your father's precious bank then?"

"At least it will still be his." Tamsin voice was quiet. "What does your father think about what you're doing?"

"I run Nethercott Bank, not him." Winchester's face was scrunched into a fierce scowl. "I make my own rules."

"As long as the Albirsion Corporation agrees." Darrogh stood and held his hand out to Tamsin. "We need to leave."

Firbin walked toward them.

"These guys won't be able to protect you," Winchester said with disdain. "You haven't a clue what you're dealing with."

Darrogh put his body in front of Tamsin. "I know exactly what I am dealing with. You are the one who doesn't realize how serious the situation is. You can tell your Albireon friends that they have Hunters on their trail now. We don't stop."

Winchester shook his head. "Do you really think they'll care?"

"Yes." Darrogh motioned Firbin to go out the back door. "I've defeated them in more than one battle, and I will do so again."

"You're not making sense." Winchester took a step back and glared at Tamsin. "Don't say I didn't warn you."

Darrogh watched Winchester walk out of the café. He still had the uneasy sensation of being watched. He did not know where it was coming from. Firbin was standing at the hallway to the back exit. Darrogh scanned the café once more and noticed a short bald man in a large overcoat. His eyes looked down when Darrogh focused on him.

There was no doubt that he'd been watching them. He seemed to be fiddling with something in his pocket.

"*Is the rear still clear?*" Darrogh asked Breanon.

"*Yes.*" Breanon's voice was matter of fact.

"*We're coming out.*"

"*Is there anyone out front Jehon?*"

"*They followed Winchester.*"

"*Maybe he is the one with the problems with the Albireons,*" Darrogh said in a dry voice. "*Meet us at the exit.*"

"*Savis bring the van to the back exit.*"

Firbin shielded Tamsin from the front and Darrogh brought up the rear. The man in the overcoat stood at the same time. Darrogh was going to find out why he was watching them. Once outside Darrogh motioned Firbin to stand to one side. He took the other side. Jehon guided Tamsin to the van which now blocked the laneway.

They waited.

It took a couple of minutes before the door was opened a fraction of an inch.

That was enough for Darrogh. He pulled the door wide and grabbed the man by his collar. Darrogh hauled him out of the café and threw him up against the wall.

"Who are you?"

"Nobody." His voice shook.

"Why were you watching us?"

The man shook his head. "I was having a cappuccino."

"What's in your pocket?" Darrogh lowered the man to his feet. "Firbin check it out."

"You can't do this," He protested in a loud voice.

Firbin pulled out a small camera. He turned it on and started to scan through the pictures. "He's been following us for some time."

Darrogh clenched his jaw. "How bad?"

"Enough to know that you guys are up to no good." The photographer jutted his chin out. "I'll take this to the police. We'll see what they have to say about you detaining an innocent man and stealing his camera."

Firbin put the camera screen in front of Darrogh. It was a picture of him carrying Tamsin away from Saxby's apartment. Darrogh clenched the man's arm and moved him to the van. He pushed him onto a seat and nodded to Savis to drive.

"This is kidnapping." The man's voice echoed throughout the van.

"I need answers." Darrogh glared at the man. "You are coming with us."

Chapter 10

Tamsin's house used to be a peaceful sanctuary.

Now it was harboring criminals.

Darrogh and his men had been here for only a week, and her life had been turned upside down. She doubted it would ever be the same again. Before they'd arrived, the most she'd ever had to worry about was a cheating fiancé. Now, she'd been involved in a killing, kidnapping, and if her father was to be believed, extortion and corporate takeovers.

Tamsin sighed and looked at the man they'd seized at the café.

He was a short, balding, nondescript person that you'd miss in a crowd. That seemed to be the problem. Her highly skilled bodyguards had overlooked him and he'd acquired information that they wanted. She leaned back into her large cushioned chair and hoped it wasn't serious. The look on Darrogh's face told her nothing.

Darrogh had an impassive, unreadable expression, yet she sensed unease and anger beneath the surface. He kept glancing at her and she swore she saw the flickering of worry in his eyes. It felt as if she was reading his thoughts more than seeing them. It was ridiculous. No one could do that.

Firbin was searching the prisoner's pockets. He pulled out a business card and handed it to Darrogh.

"Peter Newton." Darrogh glanced up from the card. "It says that you are a Private Investigator."

"That's right, and you're interfering with my work."

"Does that work mean you follow people and take photographs?" Darrogh threw the card on the table and picked up the camera.

"My client requires proof. You know what they say about a photograph."

"No, I do not." Darrogh frowned. "Explain."

"Seeing is believing?"

When Darrogh still gave him a blank look, Peter continued. "A picture's worth a thousand words?"

"There are no words in pictures." Darrogh looked down at the camera.

Tamsin hid a smile at the look of disbelief on the investigator's face. Darrogh spoke perfect English, but he didn't understand the nuances. It was as if he was still learning the language. She added that to her mental list of things she had to discuss with him.

A nerve tightened in Darrogh's jaw. "How long you have been following us?"

His harsh tone sent a shiver down her back. He looked up at her and she sensed rather than saw a flash of reassurance. She hugged her arms close to her body. She had to trust that he knew what he was doing. Her father and Winchester had been very clear about her predicament.

She was in danger.

Darrogh and his men were the only reason she was alive.

"You guys are amateurs." Peter boasted. "I've been tailing this pretty lady for months now. Things just got interesting when you appeared."

"What does that mean?" Darrogh's eyes narrowed.

"Miss Creighton stayed at home more than she went out."

Darrogh glanced over at her and she nodded. "I've kept a low profile since last year."

"When you called off your wedding." Peter cleared his throat. "That's about the same time I was hired to follow you."

"Who hired you?"

Peter shrugged. "That's confidential."

Darrogh picked Peter up by his collar and gave him a shake. "Tell us now. It is my duty to protect Tamsin and you are preventing that. Nothing gets in the way of my mission."

Peter's eyes widened. "The law protects me. I have a right to do my job without interference."

Darrogh pulled him close. "Your laws do not concern me."

Peter turned to her with a pleading look. "Tell him to stop."

Tamsin hugged herself closer. She wanted this whole sordid thing to go away, but Darrogh shook his head at her. A sense of calm came over her and even though she disagreed with what they were doing to the man, she couldn't deny that Peter had information that they need.

"You had best tell him, Mr. Newton." She forced her voice to remain steady.

A flicker of fear passed over the private investigator's face.

"I don't know." His voice was a whine.

"You have no name?" Darrogh put him back in his seat. "How do you get paid?"

"I have a mailbox that I use."

"How do you contact him?"

Peter straightened the collar of his coat. "We both use the same box. He has a key and so do I. Every evening I deposit copies of my surveillance photos in it."

"That does not sound logical." Savis spoke for the first time. "Why not electronically. That is how most people do it."

"He wants to remain anonymous." Peter shrugged. "All I care about is that he pays me."

"Where were you when these pictures were taken?" Darrogh's voice was emotionless.

"In my car. I parked in a small lot near the nightclub and waited. It was just luck the lot was across from the alleyway."

"So you saw Tamsin escape."

"And I followed her."

"Did you stay in your car?" Darrogh took a step closer to Peter.

"I wasn't about to interrupt the lovebirds."

Tamsin's stomach twisted. Something in Darrogh's tone alerted her to the seriousness of what was in those pictures. She reached her hand out for the camera. There on the viewing screen was a shot of Darrogh holding her in his arms. She was wearing his jacket and slumped back in his arms. She looked to be completely incapacitated.

The next picture showed her snuggled close to Darrogh's chest.

Contentment and peace were evident in her smile.

Her stomach fluttered when she saw the expression on Darrogh's face. He was a man who never showed emotion, yet that wasn't the case in this picture. The camera had captured him looking down at her. There was distress and concern in his gaze. If she didn't know different, she'd say it was a picture of two people in love. Her finger traced down the camera viewing screen.

She clicked through several more of the photos and found one with her getting into the car with George Saxby. The pictures were damning.

"What did you do with these photos?" Tamsin handed the camera to Firbin.

"I gave them to my client."

"That's an invasion of my privacy." Tamsin's stomach churned with nausea. "What did I ever do to you?"

"You're lucky I'm not a paparazzo. The stuff I've shot this past week would have made me a fortune."

The men froze.

Tamsin held her breath.

"What things?" Darrogh's tone was low.

Peter glanced up at him with a smile. "All the partying and clubbing. Miss Creighton's been taking you guys on a merry little run around London. I almost felt sorry for you."

Firbin waved the camera. "There are no pictures of that here."

"I had to change the memory card last night."

"Where are the other photos?"

"Back at my place." Peter shrugged. "I transfer everything to my computer."

"We will want your computer and the memory cards." Darrogh's voice was threatening.

"You can't just take them," Peter protested. "That's theft."

"I will pay you for them." Tamsin thought it was time to interrupt before this escalated into a shouting match. The heavy-handed approach wasn't going to work. Peter was a businessman and if there was one thing she knew, that was business.

"I'd also like to pay you for your services."

"I can't work for two people."

Tamsin kept her voice reasonable. "I'm offering you more money and the chance at a regular job if you work out."

Peter glanced up at Darrogh. "Do I have to be near this guy?"

"For a while, but in time I'll find a position for you at Creighton's. We always need good security people. After what I've heard and seen today, you strike me as being very ingenious."

Peter leaned back. "I can tell you're a person who appreciates good work."

Tamsin smiled. "I also reward those who work with me."

Peter's eyes narrowed. "I'm getting three thousand pounds a month, plus expenses."

"I'll pay you five thousand pounds and I'm the only person you work for." Tamsin crossed her arms. "If you double cross me, you'll answer to Darrogh."

Darrogh took his cue and leaned close. "There are penalties for lying."

Peter gulped. "I'll work for you, but not with him."

"He's the head of my personal security." Tamsin wished that Darrogh wasn't so imposing right now. As if on cue, he stepped back from Peter and walked to the window. She let out the breath she'd been holding. Now was her chance to seal the deal.

"What about a signing bonus?"

Peter took his eyes off Darrogh and looked at her. "What kind?"

"Another five thousand pounds."

"Done." The words of acceptance were out of Peter's mouth before she'd stopped speaking.

"I do have some terms." Tamsin continued. "First, we need all copies of the photos you've taken since you started following me. Second, I need you to help my security team find out who hired you."

Peter nodded. "I can give you the photos, but I don't know how you'll locate the man I was working for."

Darrogh turned away from the window. "Are you working with us?"

"Yes." Peter held up his hand. "Remember, I'm doing this willingly, so no rough stuff."

"You have my word as a Hunter." Darrogh crossed his arms over his chest.

Peter laughed. "Are you really a Hunter?"

"I do not lie."

Peter stood. "I thought you guys were an urban legend."

"We are real." Firbin grinned.

"Better working with a Hunter than against one." Peter straightened his overcoat. "Where do you want to begin?"

"Your apartment." Darrogh walked toward Peter. "We need to look at those other photos."

"What about the guy I'm working for."

"We will trap him." Darrogh nodded to Kerm and Savis. "Take him down to the van. I will be with you shortly."

Firbin, Breanon, and Jehon went into the kitchen.

Tamsin was left alone with Darrogh.

She braced herself for an argument. She clasped her hands together and stood when he approached. He might not like her interference, but this was still her house, and technically, these guys worked for her. Besides, Peter Newton was now cooperating with them.

"Can you afford to pay Mr. Newton that much money?"

Darrogh's question and concern took her by surprise.

She nodded. "He operated under your radar for a week, so he must be good. He can help you for as long as you need him and then I'll find a job for him at the Bank."

"Thank you." Darrogh hesitated for a second. "I would have retrieved the information from him."

"I gave him an incentive to help." Tamsin rolled the tension from her shoulders. "It saved time."

"Everyone on this planet wants something." Darrogh sounded cynical.

"You're being paid by my father. How is that different?"

"Your father can afford it and he offered." Darrogh held her gaze. "If you were in danger and had no money, then we would still protect you. We are here to right wrongs and provide justice."

"You hire out your services. That makes you mercenaries." Tamsin hadn't forgotten what her father was paying for her protection.

"We are warriors." Darrogh's voice was low. "We have been trained to defend and protect. We do that for anyone who is in need, not just those who can pay."

"That's not what my father suggested."

"You father is a desperate man who will do whatever he can to protect you. He heard of us and asked for our help. He does not believe in what we do." Darrogh crossed his arms over his chest. "He only cares about results."

Tamsin rubbed her forehead. Talking with Darrogh was like walking on egg shells. She didn't know what would offend or please him. It was all too much. She was tired and still feeling the aftereffects of the Rohypnol that she'd ingested the night before. She needed sleep.

"Go rest." Darrogh spoke in a soft voice. "I do not wish for you to be upset. We will talk when I return from Mr. Newton's house."

Tamsin moved toward the stairs. "I have so many questions and everything is happening too fast for me."

"I will tell you whatever you want to know."

Darrogh reached a hand out to her.

The breath caught in her throat.

She waited for his touch, anticipating the shock of awareness that would pass through her body. Instead, he dropped his arm and took a step back. His eyes searched hers for several seconds before he turned, and left the house.

Tamsin watched him until the door closed and then she headed up the stairs. Whenever he was near she felt a quivering in her stomach and a tightness in her chest. Her mouth went dry and she had to force herself to look away. She recognized the signs. She was attracted to him. It was ludicrous because he certainly hadn't given her any indication that he was interested in her. His actions suggested that the last place he wanted to be was near her.

That's not how he'd looked in the picture.

The way he'd held her close and the concern on his face were at odds with his usual behavior. Tamsin picked up a throw and stretched out on the settee in her bedroom. None of the men had shown any interest in women. She'd dragged them around to enough nightclubs this past week to know. Women threw themselves at the men, but they ignored them.

It was a wonderful quality in a bodyguard, but abnormal behavior for a man.

That wasn't the only strange thing that she wanted to discuss with Darrogh. He spoke of Earth as if he was separate from it. He referred to it as this planet. What other planet was there? It made no sense. As soon as the men returned from Peter's house with the photos, she would insist that Darrogh explain.

Another remark had caught her attention.

Peter mentioned that the Hunters were an urban legend? Tamsin grabbed her laptop and typed in Hunters. The usual information about animals and equipment came up. She then tried Hunter protection and that's when she saw the website aHunter4Hire.com.

A shiver went up her back when she read the comments that people had written. Most were treating it as a joke, but there were some testimonials that sounded very real. Stories of being rescued from kidnappers, lives being saved, and murders avenged.

It was not the website of a security company.

This was a site for vigilante justice.

Chapter 11

Peter Newton lived in a studio flat that was large enough to contain his computer equipment, and little else. Darrogh looked at the cluttered room and fought back his frustration. It would take time to sort through everything and find evidence that led to the people who were threatening Tamsin and her father. Peter's photos were their best chance of doing that.

It was worth the effort.

"Where are the pictures?"

"You're impatient," Peter muttered as he moved his cat off a large table and turned on his computer. "I told you I had everything in order."

Darrogh hoped it was better organized than his flat. The orange cat sidled up to him and rubbed against his leg. He did not comprehend why humans insisted on letting animals live with them. He could understand if they were using them for sustenance, but that was not the case with cats.

"Here they are." Peter spoke from behind a large monitor. "I've been following Miss Creighton long before you came on the scene."

"We need to see everything from the beginning of your surveillance." Darrogh motioned for Savis to go to the computer. "There may be something in the pictures that you have missed."

"I doubt it." Peter pushed away from his desk and let Savis take over. "Do you want anything to drink? I have tea."

Darrogh shook his head. "Where are the written instructions that your client left you?"

Peter took off his coat and tossed it on his futon before going into the small alcove that served as a kitchenette. He filled a kettle with water and plugged it in. "I threw everything out. The envelopes were hand delivered to the postal box, so there were no stamps on them that would have helped with locating where they were mailed from."

Darrogh started shifting through a pile of printed photos that were on a side table. "Are these from your investigation of Tamsin?"

Peter shook his head. "Not really. I took a few photos of the bank. It's a pretty famous institution. The building dates back to the Victorian age."

"Is that old?" Kerm had sat beside Darrogh and was leafing through another stack of photos."

"Old enough." Peter shut off the kettle and poured boiling water into a floral china teapot. "Is the stuff on your website true?"

"A Hunter does not betray his word," Kerm said. "We do not lie."

"How about exaggerating the truth a bit." Peter searched through his dish-cluttered countertop for a mug and rinsed it. "Some of the feats that your previous clients claim seem impossible."

"An exaggeration would be a lie."

Peter filled his mug with tea and pulled up a wooden chair to sit on. "You're very literal. Do you see everything as black or white?"

"We see all colors." Darrogh frowned down at a photo. "If we were defective, we would have been killed at birth."

Peter choked on his tea. "You're kidding?"

Darrogh shook his head. "A warrior cannot be physically flawed. Hunters have been bred and trained to fight. If we are unable to do that, then there is no reason for us to live."

Peter looked over at Kerm. "Is that what you believe?"

"We are brothers." Kerm's voice was gruff. "What is true for one, is true for all."

"You guys take this soldier stuff seriously." Peter nodded. "I wanted to enlist in the army, but they said I didn't meet the height requirements."

"Then you understand the need to be physically perfect." Darrogh shoved the picture in his hand at Peter. "Where did you take this?"

Peter squinted. "That was in the back alley behind Creighton's. It used to be the mews. Now there are little shops and restaurants that cater to the office workers."

"These men stand out." Darrogh pointed to two men with dark coats, sunglasses, and fedora hats."

"They do seem a bit unusual."

"When did you take it?"

Peter shook his head. "There's no date stamp on it, but I probably have it in the computer."

"Why did you print this one?"

Peter pointed to a figure in the foreground. "Sir Robert Creighton had walked outside with another man. I thought I might be able to sell the photo. None of the papers were interested."

"Sir Robert is with his assistant, Henry Kingsley."

"If you say so." Peter handed the picture back to Darrogh. "I never met the man."

"What about the men in black?"

Peter started to laugh. "Don't tell me you think this has something to do with aliens and UFO's."

"Why is that funny?" Savis looked up from the computer.

"It's ridiculous." Peter snorted. "How would they get here?"

"On a ship." Darrogh's voice was dry. "This is not the only inhabited planet in the universe."

Peter stopped laughing and looked from one of them to the other. "You're serious."

Darrogh did not bother answering. Humans were egotistical enough to believe that they were the only intelligent life form in the universe. It was a mistake. That was what had made them so vulnerable to the Albireons. Their presence on the planet was shrouded in secrecy and that would lead to the destruction of the human race.

He stood and passed the photo in his hand to Savis. "Find the date on this one."

"It is not the only one showing them."

"The men dressed in black?" Peter put his tea down and went over to the computer.

Darrogh watched as Savis brought up dozens of photos with the same men in them. There was no mistaking what he was looking at. Partlan, another Hunter, had recently escaped from the clutches of men dressed exactly like this.

They were not human.

They were Albireons in disguise.

Darrogh pointed at one of the pictures. "Did you realize you were being followed?"

Peter's mouth had dropped open. "I can't believe I didn't notice them."

"They did not want to be seen."

Savis hit a button and another screen pulled up dozens of more photos. There was a man in each shot, always several hundred feet away from Tamsin. It was Henry Kingsley, Creighton's assistant.

"It cannot be a coincidence that he is frequently near Tamsin." Darrogh fought to keep his voice normal. Anger that Henry Kingsley had been so close to Tamsin ripped through his body. He should have realized that Sir Robert's assistant might be more involved than they had suspected.

"These were taken before we came to London." Savis's voice was low. He looked up at Darrogh, "This past week he has not been near. We did not miss him."

"Good. Continue looking for patterns of people near her." Darrogh exhaled through gritted teeth. "We need to do better in the future."

"I looked at these pictures every day and I didn't notice." Peter swatted Darrogh on the back. "From what I've seen, you guys are taking good care of her, especially last night."

Darrogh flinched at Peter's words. It was a reminder of how he had failed to protect Tamsin. She had nearly died. They thought they had covered their tracks and now there were photos showing them at Saxby's building.

Those pictures had to be found and destroyed.

"Last night did not happen." Darrogh's voice was serious.

Peter took a step back and nodded. "Understood. I already sent those photos off. What happens to them is out of my hands."

"We will need to trap your client." Darrogh crossed his arms. "He is a threat to Tamsin's safety."

"You're the boss." Peter shook his head. "I don't know how you plan on doing that, though."

"You will leave him a message that you need to meet."

Peter shrugged. "That might work. Then what?"

"Once we know who he is, we will take care of him."

Peter frowned as he looked at each of the men. "I hope you don't plan to kill him."

Darrogh shook his head. "He will only die if he threatens us."

"He might be angry that I've trapped him. What if he comes after me?"

"We will protect you."

"That won't help if I'm dead."

"Are you refusing to meet him?" Darrogh held back his anger. "You agreed to do that for Tamsin."

"I agreed to help find the person. That doesn't mean we need a face to face." Peter ran a hand over his bald head. "Why don't I leave a note for him and we'll watch the mailbox to see who picks it up?"

Darrogh considered Peter's plan. It might work. They needed more than the person's identity, though.

"We have to meet with this person to ensure that they will not hurt Tamsin."

"We can set up a camera outside." Peter suggested. "Once we have their face, we will be able to identify them."

"That will not tell us who opens the box." Kerm's voice was quiet. "We need a camera on the box itself."

Peter sank back in his chair. "I have small remote cameras. I could set one up inside the mailbox."

"He will see it when he reaches for your note." Darrogh shook his head. "The camera has to be located where the box is visible."

"I could hide the camera on the underside of the checkout counter," Peter suggested. "A remote signal will tell us who it is and then you can follow them."

Darrogh nodded.

It was a good plan.

"Copy those photos onto a memory stick and then erase them from Peter's computer."

"Hey," Peter objected. "Those are my livelihood."

"Tamsin is paying you a bonus for them. We can do as we wish."

Peter grimace. "I've nothing to show for all of my time."

"You have been paid by your client and by Tamsin." Darrogh raised an eyebrow. "That is more than enough for an honorable man."

Peter sighed. "Why do you guys make so much sense? Just make sure you leave all the rest of the photos on the computer."

"I have done so." Savis stood. "It is time to contact your client."

"Write him that you have something that needs to be handed to him in person." Darrogh advised. "If we miss him at the mailbox, then we can catch him at your meeting."

Peter jotted down a message on a piece of paper then he shoved his arms into his overcoat. "You better know what you're doing. The last thing I need is a bullet in my head."

The ride to the mailbox rental business was quick. It was close to Peter's flat. When they had stopped the van, Savis pulled out a small button camera and handed it to Peter.

"Attach this to the underside of the countertop." He pointed to a paper cover on the bottom. "Take the paper off and it will stick to anything. Aim it at your box."

Peter grabbed the small device. "This isn't the first time I've planted a hidden camera."

"It is the first time we are trusting you to do it." Darrogh looked at Peter. "Savis will make certain that the feed is working. Do you have the message?"

Peter patted his upper jacket pocket. "I'm ready."

Darrogh nodded. "Kerm will go in with you."

"*Watch that he does not signal anyone.*" Darrogh commanded Kerm through mind connect.

When the two men had left the van, Darrogh turned to Savis. "Will this work?"

"Yes." Savis pointed to the monitor. "The camera is already transmitting."

"Good." Darrogh leaned his head against the side of the vehicle. "I cannot believe that we missed Peter last night. I was responsible for keeping her safe, and now there are photos of us leaving Saxby's building."

Savis cleared his throat. "Those pictures of you carrying Tamsin were telling. The team has suspected that you were affected by her for a while, but those shots show it clearly."

Darrogh was not surprised that his behavior was causing his fellow Hunters concern. He had been wrestling with his strange awareness and attraction to Tamsin for days now. Last night had been the turning point for him. He could no longer deny that she had a hold on him.

"I have no wish to be pair bonded." Darrogh did not hide his hesitancy. "I truly believe it is wrong for a Hunter to be with a woman."

"You are not the first to have this happen." Savis's voice was quiet. "Bonding is not meant to be a burden."

"It is for me." Darrogh clenched his hands into fists. "I have spent my life on the front lines and in constant battle. What do I know about women?"

"I do not believe any man understands women." Savis punched a few strokes into the computer. "Part of the bonding is learning to appreciate each other."

"You think I should accept this?"

"I do not think you have a choice." Savis's voice was solemn. "We are only bonded with one and it is beyond our control."

"True." Darrogh only had to remember how hard he had fought the attraction to know that it was not his decision. "It is time I had a talk with Tamsin to see how she feels."

"That is best."

"I will tell the team once I know for certain."

Darrogh's chest tightened as he considered having to reveal any of this to Tamsin, or the rest of his team. He had scoffed at Ardal, their leader, when he had announced that he had mated. Now, it was his turn to admit that pair bonding was a reality for Hunters on Earth.

Just then, the van door opened and Peter and Kerm jumped in.

"Everything is set." Kerm started the engine and pulled away from the curb. "I will drive around to be certain that we have a signal from a distance."

When they were positive that the camera was transmitting, Darrogh went back to Tamsin's house. The men at the house needed rest if they were going to be doing surveillance on the mailbox tomorrow. Peter stayed with Kerm and Savis in the van. They intended to park down the street from the drop box, and wait for the client to appear.

When he opened the house door, Tamsin was waiting for him. It was as if she had known he was close. He had barely closed the door behind him, when she grabbed his arm. A shock of intense awareness passed through him.

Tamsin's eyes widened.

She had felt it too.

"We need to talk."

Chapter 12

"What was that?" Tamsin rubbed her hands together.

Darrogh's body still tingled from touching Tamsin. "I can explain."

"I hope so." Tamsin led him up the stairs to the second floor lounge attached to her bedroom. She sat on the settee and motioned for him to take a seat in the wingback chair across from her. "Did you find what you wanted at Peter's house?"

Darrogh looked at the chair and then walked to the window. He needed to distance himself. He and his team had failed to properly monitor the people around Tamsin. The consequences of such an oversight could have been death. Despite finding Peter, disaster still might happen. Until they located the person that the photos had been given to, and retrieved the evidence, Tamsin was not safe.

"Peter had been following you long before we took over your security. His photos were very revealing."

"It sounds bad." Tamsin curled her legs under her body and leaned back.

Darrogh looked at her. "I did not protect you properly. I fear it may have been because I am unfamiliar with the ways of women."

"I'm tired of hearing things that don't make any sense to me." Tamsin's voice was filled with exasperation. "You talk about humans and Earth as if you don't belong. What does being a member of a security team called Hunters have to do with whether you can be near women?"

"We are not just security people." Darrogh struggled to find the right words to explain. "We are warriors."

"So you were soldiers and now you're civilians. Even soldiers are allowed to be with women."

"Not Hunters." Darrogh's gaze did not waver from her.

He sensed her confusion and frustration.

It was time he told Tamsin who he was.

Tamsin sighed. "It's like we're speaking two different languages."

Darrogh cleared his throat. "Before I came to Earth, I had only been on battlefields and combat frontlines. I was transferred into the unit that guarded the High Council of Cygnus, one week before execution orders were issued. I do not know how to speak to women."

"You are only making it more confusing." Tamsin held up her hands. "One thing at a time. What do you mean before you came to Earth?"

"I was born and bred on Cygnus. It is a planet in the Barnard Galaxy."

"You're from another planet?" Tamsin's voice was filled with doubt. "Does my Father know this?"

"He did not ask." Most people did not want to know where Hunters were from. Tamsin was different. He could not fight his connection with her. She needed to understand everything.

"So it's a don't ask, don't tell, policy." Tamsin's voice was filled with sarcasm.

"We live in secret."

"I'm not stupid." Tamsin rolled her eyes. "You're taller than most men and very muscular, but you're still human. Your hair is dark and your eyes black. You have two arms, two legs, and one head. You look like every other man on this planet."

"We share the same genes as humans."

"But you don't come from Earth." Tamsin's tone was dry. "This is a fascinating fantasy as far-fetched as it is fantastic. You believe you're an alien from outer space who shares the same genes as humans."

"It is the truth." Darrogh struggled to keep his voice steady.

Tamsin shut her eyes for a second. "How long have you been on Earth?"

"We crash landed here a year ago." Darrogh walked toward Tamsin.

"Why didn't you go home?" Tamsin tapped her fingers on the back of the settee. "If you're able to travel through space and come to Earth, you must have the technology to leave."

He sat on the chair across from her.

"There was a civil war on our planet."

"Let me guess, you were on the losing side." Tamsin rubbed her forehead.

"We were ordered executed because the Kaladin were defeated." Darrogh clenched his hands into fists as he remembered the devastation the war had caused. "The Holman took over the planet and decreed that all Hunters, and our genes, be destroyed. We were being transported to our deaths when we crashed."

Tamsin frowned. "Genocide is pretty extreme. Why would they do that?"

"Hunters were bred to protect and obey the Kaladin."

"So these Holman thought that you would continue fighting against them?" Tamsin brushed a strand of hair off her face. "Why not banish you?"

"We are too dangerous to ignore." Darrogh's voice was low. "We have been bred to defend. We excel at it."

"You could be trained to do other work."

"There is no other task for us. We are an ancient warrior race that has been genetically modified." Darrogh lifted his chin. "We are the best soldiers in the universe."

Tamsin shook her head. "That's like saying you're the prettiest woman in the galaxy because you won Miss Universe."

"I have fought on many worlds and defeated numerous enemies. I know that Hunters are feared and respected by all."

"If you're from another planet then there is no way you could have human genes." Tamsin looked pleased with her logic.

"We came from Earth originally." He clenched his jaw in an effort to remain calm. He had to convince Tamsin about Hunters, otherwise she would never believe him about the Albireons.

"So you were humans that were abducted by the Kaladin?"

"Eons ago." Darrogh kept his voice steady. "It was so long ago that all knowledge of Earth had been stripped from our collective memories. We did not know about this planet or our connection to it."

"Do you understand how difficult this is to believe?" Tamsin stopped fidgeting with her hair. "You're bigger than most men, but you still look human."

"We were modified and altered to be warriors. Fighting is all we are used for. We do not have children or mates like other men."

"Never?"

"It is forbidden. We guard women and fight their wars, but we have no other contact with them."

"You've never been with a woman?" Tamsin sat on the edge of the settee. "I find that hard to believe. Men are not known for their celibacy, especially when women would be eager to spend time with you."

"Hunters are not like other men." Darrogh sensed Tamsin's beginning acceptance of who he was. "That is why it is difficult for us to be around women."

"Why agree to protect me then?" Tamsin frowned. "I've given you more than enough reasons to refuse the job."

"You needed help," Darrogh said. "That is what we do."

"But now you have doubts."

"When I accepted the assignment, I had no connection with you. I did not believe that bonding was possible." Darrogh leaned closer to Tamsin. "I understand fighting and war. Since crashing on Earth, we have found that things are different here. I do not trust the changes that this planet has made to us."

"How is it different?"

Darrogh's stomach tightened at the thought of revealing the secrets of his abilities. Silence was what had given his race the advantage in battle and it had kept them alive on this planet. If the connection between him and Tamsin was strengthening then it would not be long before she realized everything about him. He had to trust Tamsin with the truth.

"This planet affects our metabolism. We have quicker reflexes and keener senses, and we live longer."

Tamsin put up her hand. "You only crashed here a year ago. You can't possibly know that."

"There are other Hunters who have been on this planet for thirty years. They were stranded here when they were children. Kerm is one of them."

"Kerm doesn't look thirty."

"He is older than me." Darrogh clasped his hands in front of him. "He has had to hide from humans in order to survive. That has given him many talents that have made our transition to this Earth easier."

"How old are you?" Tamsin's voice was quiet.

"I have seen thirty-two summers. Seventeen of those years have been on the battlefield."

"That means you started fighting at fifteen." Tamsin shook her head. "Why would your parents allow that?"

"Hunters are bred in birthing chambers. We do not have parents."

"This is insane." Tamsin's voice cracked. "So you work as mercenaries now."

"We right wrongs on this planet." He sensed Tamsin's disbelief.

"I'm surprised you don't hire yourself out to governments if your skills are as good as you say."

"The older Hunters did that in the past." Darrogh grimaced as he remembered what the others had done to survive. "Now they fight with honor and for justice."

"Because that is better than fighting for a country?" Tamsin's voice was scornful. "None of this makes sense."

Darrogh leaned back in his chair. "It is important that you understand and believe what I am telling you if we are going to continue to protect you."

"You were protecting me before. What has changed?" Tamsin's voice held a hint of suspicion.

Darrogh clenched his jaw. "There is one thing I have not told you about Hunters."

Tamsin tilted her head. "From the tone of your voice, I assume this is the reason we're having this discussion."

"One of the reasons." Darrogh nodded. "I told you that our genes had been manipulated and modified to make us the best warriors possible. Along with strength, we were also bred to be focused and dedicated."

"That makes sense."

"These abilities affected how we react to women. That is why it is forbidden for a Hunter to mate."

Tamsin's eyes widened. "Are you telling me that you're abusive?"

Darrogh considered letting her believe the worse of him. It would ensure that she kept her distance and decrease the likelihood of their bonding. Honor and truth would not allow a falsehood to stand between them.

"Any harm against a woman or child is punishable by death. That is the first law of the Sacred Code which I have defended my whole life."

Tamsin's shoulders sagged. "For a second, you had me worried. So you're protective of women. That's not a cause for concern."

"We protect and obey women." Darrogh hesitated as he struggled to find the right words. "Even though we were forbidden to mate, we have legends from ancient times when it was allowed."

"There must have been a reason to prohibit it."

"A Hunter forms a pair bond with one woman." Darrogh's voice was filled with sincerity. "We have found that this connection is absolute and complete."

Tamsin raised her eyebrows. "You said that Hunters don't mate."

"Things have changed since we came to Earth." Darrogh pulled up the sleeve on his left arm and exposed a small scar. "Our implants were removed so that we could not be pursued.

Tamsin nodded. "They were tracking devices."

"They boosted our skills and inhibited us from mating."

"They made you impotent." Tamsin's voice held acceptance. "Without the implant, you are attracted to women. That doesn't seem to be a problem."

"You do not fully understand about pair bonding." Darrogh tried to keep his voice calm. "Hunters are not casually available to women like most men on your planet. There is only one pair bond for a Hunter. Not even death can break the link. His mate is the most important thing in his life. He will disobey orders if it means protecting her, and he will never bond or mate with another woman."

Tamsin's eyes widened. "That's why it was forbidden for you to mate."

"Nothing is more powerful than the connection between mates. They think as one and they communicate on a level that is unique."

"It sounds intense." Tamsin's eyes never left his face. "Why does this concern me?"

"I am bonding with you."

Chapter 13

"And I'm not the woman you desire." Tamsin forced her voice to remain calm.

It was clear that Darrogh didn't want her. Otherwise, he wouldn't be so upset. What was it about men? At least he was telling her before they became involved. That was more honest than Winchester had ever been.

"You are the only woman who is right for me." Darrogh's voice sounded tortured.

"What's the problem then?"

"I do not know if I can trust how I feel." Darrogh clenched his hands into fists. "This planet has had a strange effect on us. Others of my unit have found their pair bond and mated, so there is truth in the legends. I still believe that a Hunter should not let anything interfere with his ability to fight."

As rejections went, this one was unique.

She was a magnet for men unable to commit. It had to be a personality flaw that they sensed. Darrogh's reason for rejecting her was unbelievable. He was taller and more muscular than most men, and had rugged good looks. She was drawn to his aura of suppressed power. The only drawback was that he was constantly on alert and always in control.

He was like no other man she had ever met.

It was just her luck that he thought he was from another planet and didn't want her. There was no doubt that Darrogh believed what he was saying. How could she possibly accept such a wild story? It sounded as if he'd lost touch with reality. Was it even safe to be alone with him?

"I would never harm you."

Tamsin's eyes widened. "You keep anticipating what I'm thinking."

"It is part of the bonding." Darrogh dropped his head in his hands. "I do not think there is any way to stop it."

"Deciphering my facial expressions is what you call bonding?" Tamsin's snapped out the words. She was tired of his parlor tricks. "I'm not that easy to read."

"I hear your thoughts and sense your emotions." Darrogh looked up. "The others explained the pair bonding, but I never thought it would be like this."

"How do you hear my thoughts?" Tamsin's tone was hesitant.

"Your doubts and questions are in my head." Darrogh's voice was low. "It is like the mind connect between Hunters, and it has the power to reach inside of me and twist. Your voice is all I want to hear."

"This is what your pair bonding is about? Telecommunication?"

Darrogh shook his head. "That is only part of it. The bonding is a complete joining of body and mind."

"I don't want anybody crawling around in my head." A shiver went through Tamsin. What irrational rants had Darrogh been listening to? It was an invasion of her privacy.

"Your thoughts are never indiscreet." Darrogh smiled. "You have the power to block the pair bonding if you wish."

"I wish." Tamsin sat back and crossed her arms. "It's not right for people to hear someone's thoughts."

"It is not a bad thing." Darrogh's tone was thoughtful. "I knew you were in danger when you left with Saxby. I could hear your cry for help and feel your desperation. I was out of my mind with the need to find you before that monster put his hands on you."

"You reached me in time." Tamsin pushed back her memories of that evening.

"I was too late. He had already hit you." Darrogh's hands clenched into fists. "It took all of my years of training to refrain from killing him right away. I had to make certain that you were being held against your will."

"How could you even think that I wanted that?"

Darrogh shrugged. "I have seen much on this planet. For some people, that would have been pleasure."

Tamsin looked out the window. "You're right."

"At the time, I could not trust that I had read your thoughts correctly. My response to seeing you hurt, may have caused harm. I reacted in haste and was careless." Darrogh shook his head. "That is why I think it would be better if I put some distance between us. I want to protect you, yet how can I, if I hesitate or overreact."

Tamsin turned back to Darrogh. "You say you're an alien who has feelings for me and that interferes with your work. Who protects me when you've left?"

"One of the others will take charge."

"And what happens if they decide that they are bonding with me and they want to leave?" Tamsin could have cried at how ridiculous the situation was. "No member of your team will want to guard me."

"You do not understand the nature of the pair bond." Darrogh leaned toward her. "We only bond once. There is no attraction to other women."

Tamsin frowned. "So none of the other men in your team will connect with me?"

"No." Darrogh grimaced. "I am not even certain about you bonding with me."

"I get that you don't want to be near me. You don't have to keep repeating it."

Darrogh took her hand.

A shock of electricity raced through her fingers.

"You are wrong. All I desire is to be with you. It consumes me and is a fire that burns within me. My every thought is filled with you, whether it is about your safety, plans to protect you, or just to be near you."

"That sounds a lot like love."

Darrogh's gaze was intense. "I do not sense that you feel the same way."

"How do you know?"

"You would be able to hear my thoughts too." Darrogh let her hand go. "That is why I am uncertain about what is happening to me."

"Are you telling me that the mind reading goes both ways?"

"Of course." Darrogh sounded surprised. "How else can it be a joining unless both partners are able to link to each other?"

"How is that possible?" Tamsin's voice held a tremor.

"A pair bond is the true connection between two people who are meant to be together. There is no other person that they will ever bond with in this way."

"So they are in perfect synch?"

"Yes." Darrogh sighed. "Now do you understand why I doubt what is happening to me? It should not be one-sided."

Tamsin clenched her hands together. "It's not."

Darrogh's eyes narrowed. "What are you saying?"

"When I was Saxby's prisoner and couldn't move, I saw you clearly in my head." Tamsin hesitated for a second. "You told me you'd be there soon."

"Why did you not tell me?"

"I was drugged and my memory was foggy." Tamsin's fingers fluttered against the cheek that Saxby had hit. "I thought it was a hallucination."

"Was there anything else?"

"A couple of times I felt a sense of calm overcome me. Is that the kind of thing you're talking about?"

Darrogh nodded.

"So what does this mean?" Tamsin's voice rose. "Are we fated to be joined? In case you haven't noticed, I don't want to let another man into my life. How can I trust that you won't leave me like Winchester did?"

"Winchester has no honor," Darrogh scoffed. "Once a Hunter has bonded, there is no one else for him. It is a physical pain to be separated."

Darrogh believed what he was telling her, but did she? She might sense when he was near, yet that didn't mean she was reading his thoughts. She was attracted to him, and her body hummed with sparks when he touched her. Dare she trust that?

"What do we do now?" Her voice was a low whisper.

"I have always considered the bonding a curse because it lessens a warrior's focus. Now, I am not so certain." Darrogh's tone was reflective. "I am focused on ensuring your protection. It has made me more effective as your bodyguard. My concern is what will happen once you do not need my services."

"You said the connection lasts a lifetime."

"A woman can refuse the mating. I would be bound to obey." Darrogh winced. "The pain of not being with you would be unbearable."

"Do you always do what a woman asks?"

"Yes." Darrogh's tone was solemn. "Women are obeyed. It is a man's duty to serve her."

Tamsin opened her mouth and then shut it.

Darrogh was serious.

Finally, she asked, "Is this something that Hunters have been bred to do?"

"All men on Cygnus obey women. They are the ones that rule and make the decisions."

"I asked numerous times in the past week to be left alone, and you didn't do it."

"Women on earth are not used to ruling. A Hunter obeys unless it is a matter of safety. I deemed that you still needed protection. That is why I refused your requests."

"So you don't think I can rule?"

Darrogh grinned. "You are a very competent women. I believe we know more about security than you."

"Well I can't argue with that." Tamsin shook her head. "I almost got myself killed yesterday."

"It will not happen again." Darrogh stood. "There is more at stake here than we first thought. We have proof that the Albireons are responsible for the threats on your life."

"Who exactly are the Albireons?" Tamsin asked. "I know they're in control of the corporation that is trying to take my father's bank. You seem to have a past history with them. Have others been threatened by them?"

"They are the scourge of the universe." Darrogh's tone was disdainful. "They take over planets, strip them of their resources and genes, and then, they destroy them. They have been on Earth for several years and have infiltrated your governments to the highest levels."

Tamsin frowned. "Are you saying they're aliens also?"

"Yes." Darrogh crossed his arms. "I have fought them in numerous battles. They have no honor and deceive with every promise. They are no match for a Hunter. Since we discovered their presence on this planet, we have looked for a means to eradicate them."

"Why threaten my father?"

"They need economic control and his bank is part of the plan. We were unaware of how deep their influence on this planet was." Darrogh's jaw clenched. "They have more power than we thought. It will be difficult to defeat them."

Tamsin wasn't sure what she thought about this latest development. She had just accepted that Darrogh was probably telling the truth about being from another planet. Now he was asking her to believe that there was an alien conspiracy to overtake Earth. This morning, her biggest concern was trying to forget that she'd almost been raped and killed. Now, the world was at risk of being destroyed.

"It is a lot to accept."

Tamsin smiled. "Reading my thoughts again?"

Darrogh nodded. "I have been in numerous battles with Albireons. I have seen many of my brothers killed because of the treachery of this race. I do not wish to see any more deaths."

"Is my father at risk from them?"

"Once they have his bank, they will have no further use for him."

Tamsin's heart skipped a beat.

Her father was all she had.

"How can we protect him?" Tamsin didn't care what it took, she wanted her father alive. If these Albireons were truly behind the threats, then she wanted them killed.

"He is safe as long as he controls Creighton's." Darrogh's gaze burned with intensity. "You are the one in danger. Your father's greatest weakness is his love for you, and they are using that against him. If you are safe, he will have no need to give them the bank."

"So keeping me alive is the best way to thwart them?"

Darrogh nodded. "Your safety is my only concern."

The enormity of what she'd just learned was suffocating. She wanted her world to stop spinning and the stress to lessen. Darrogh was looking at her with a hooded expression, but she could feel his uncertainty. He had risked exposure by telling her the truth about himself and she was thankful. It was a relief to know that she hadn't been hallucinating.

The bond he spoke of sounded serious.

She needed playfulness and joy in her life too.

Tamsin went to Darrogh. He stood rigid and unmoving. Now that he'd told her about his beliefs, she knew that where she was concerned at least, he was not indifferent. She rubbed her hand up his arm, enjoying the sparks of fire that burned between them.

"You're the only man I want guarding me." She reached up and stroked down his cheek. "You will just have to overcome your aversion to having me near."

"That is not what I said." Darrogh's voice was hoarse.

Tamsin batted her eyes. "You threatened to leave."

"I do not trust these feelings."

"I don't trust men, but I've made an exception in your case." Tamsin walked over to her dressing table.

"Why are you deliberately misleading me?" Darrogh's voice was filled with confusion.

"It's called flirting and it's fun."

The tension eased out of Darrogh's shoulders. "You are not upset by what I have told you."

Tamsin picked up her brush. "You said we are bonding, so you already know what I am feeling."

"You wish to play?" Darrogh tilted his head. "Now is the time for planning."

Tamsin leaned back against her dresser. "What's the point of this pair bond if there isn't any fun?"

"I did not say that."

"So far all you've told me about is having to protect and guard me." Tamsin "I crave happiness and pleasure in my life."

Darrogh frowned. "I do not understand."

"You've spent your whole life fighting and that is all you're focused on." Tamsin took a deep breath. Somehow, she had to make Darrogh understand that there were other things in life besides war. "A couple share the good and the bad times."

"You are not concerned by the Albireons or their threats."

"I've decided that you can do the worrying for both of us." Tamsin pointed the brush at him. "I trust you to protect me. I will do whatever you decide."

Darrogh took a step toward her.

A knock on the door stopped him.

"Come," Darrogh barked.

Firbin opened the door. "Kerm has reported activity at the stakeout."

Chapter 14

"We had a pickup, but it was not Peter's client." Savis showed Darrogh the video playback on the computer.

Darrogh watched as a young man in a black hoodie, opened the mailbox and took out Peter's envelope. He kept his back to the countertop so there was no chance to see his face. He opened the note, and then left the building.

"Is that all?"

"We followed him and were able to get some photos." Savis clicked on the shots. "He called someone after leaving, and then threw the phone away."

"It was probably a disposable cell at the other end."

Darrogh kept his frustration in check. When he and Breanon had arrived at the van, he had expected to find out who the client was. He wanted this man found so that he could ensure Tamsin's safety. The sooner that was done, the better. If he stayed much longer with Tamsin, he would never leave her side.

"That is what we thought." Savis continued to scroll through the photos. "We followed him for over an hour. He led us nowhere."

"He went into a pub and was buying rounds." Kerm added. "He had lots of money to spend."

"So he was paid to make the pickup and call with the information." Darrogh felt like gnashing his teeth.

"Probably." Peter looked down at his watch. "It's a good thing I arranged to meet up with the client in person. I said eleven tonight at the Joy of Life Fountain, in Hyde Park. It should be private at that time."

"How will you recognize him?" Darrogh turned to Peter.

"I just assumed that he'd know me because he hired me. I said I'd be sitting on the edge of the fountain. Nobody's there at night." Peter's voice was hesitant. "Did I do wrong?"

"No. We will monitor everyone who is at the fountain. We have two hours to prepare." Darrogh motioned to Savis to drive. "We will go now and find a vantage point to observe you."

"What am I supposed to tell him?" Peter's voice was unsteady. "I don't have any photos from today because you guys took them."

"Tell him your cover was blown, and you cannot work for him anymore." Darrogh said.

"I'll add that you guys took my camera." Peter chuckled. "At least that's the truth."

"Ask for money." Savis looked up from his computer screen. "That way he will not suspect a trap."

Peter nodded. "Good idea."

There was silence as they drove to Edgware Street and then east along Park Lane, looking for a parking space close to the Fountain. A quick surveillance of the area showed paved pathways and lights. The only real cover they would have was the darkness of night. The strategist in Darrogh did not like the location. It was not ideal for a covert operation.

They parked the van some distance away from the fountain.

Darrogh, Savis, and Peter walked the area.

It was a cool, summer evening and the moon was bright in the sky. There was very little cloud cover, and with the streetlights and moon, the area was too bright for them to go unseen. The fountain's spouting water and its dancing, bronze statues were illuminated with blue-tinted floodlights. The buildings across from the park, and the road, provided enough additional light that a person could almost read by it. If someone was watching the grounds, they would be spotted right away.

"Why would you choose this place?" Savis was looking around at the open area surrounding the fountain.

"It's easy to get to, and safe." Peter shrugged. "He won't try anything out in the open."

"Good." Darrogh patted the front of Peter's jacket. "You will have to wear a microphone and camera because we will not be able to get close enough to protect you."

"You said I'd be guarded."

They returned to the van.

"You picked the location." Darrogh motioned for Savis to take over. "If this is someone who has been following Tamsin, then they will recognize us."

Once inside the vehicle, Peter unbuttoned his shirt and let Savis wrap a wire around him. When that was finished, a small camera similar to the one they had used for the mailbox, was placed on the underside of his shirt collar.

"That should give us the information we need." Darrogh gave Peter a nod of approval. "Remember you are angry because you have lost your equipment. Do not give him a chance to think about anything else."

"Right." Peter straightened his shoulders. "If I get some money out of this, great."

"The important thing is for us to see who it is." Darrogh's voice was firm. "Do not try and get any evidence. Tell him and then leave."

"The sooner you are back at the van, the quicker we can find out who your client is," Savis added.

"You guys could ruin my reputation if anyone finds out I've helped you." Peter ran his hand under his collar. "There's such a thing as confidentiality agreements."

"You have never met the person so he could not have signed a contract." Darrogh's voice was dry. "That alone should have alerted you to the fact that this was not an honest operation."

"It's hard being a private investigator." Peter's voice rose defensively. "I take the work where I can find it."

"That is why you are helping us. Tamsin has agreed to find a position for you at the bank." Darrogh turned to Savis. "Is the equipment ready?"

"Yes."

Darrogh opened the van door. "It is time for you to leave."

Peter looked down at his watch. "I still have an hour."

"It is better for you to be in place before he arrives." Darrogh's voice was firm. "We do not want him seeing you leaving this van."

Peter sighed. "It's a good thing it's a nice night."

"We will be listening. If there is a problem, we will come." Darrogh waited until Peter was outside before continuing. "We will follow your mystery client after the meeting, so you need to get back here fast."

"Or you'll leave me?"

"Exactly."

"I was kidding," Peter protested. "You can't abandon me."

"We move fast. If you want to work with us, then you better keep up."

Peter nodded. "If I miss my ride, I'll meet you back at Tamsin's house."

Darrogh watched Peter until he reached the fountain and then he slid the van door closed. Soon, he would find out who was having Tamsin followed. Hopefully, that would lead to the people who were threatening her life. It would be the longest hour of his life. When he turned back to his men, they looked up from their work with solemn expressions.

They deserved to know the truth.

He cleared his throat and sat. "You have questions."

Breanon went back to examining his rifle. "You will tell us when you are ready."

"I do not know if that will ever happen." Darrogh's voice was gruff. "I am forming a bond with Tamsin."

"You sound as if this is a bad thing." Savis's voice was matter of fact.

"I do not trust the effects this planet has on us."

"You're still new to Earth. In time, your body will adjust." Kerm spoke in a quiet voice.

"You have been here thirty years." Darrogh looked at the other man. "How have you reacted to being near women?"

"They've never affected me." Kerm's voice was devoid of emotion. "Until your unit arrived, we never considered the possibility of finding a mate."

"Ardal accepted his bonding." Savis's tone was one of reason. "So have Niail and Partlan. There is no shame in admitting that you have formed a pair bond."

"Catal denied his mate, and that caused him pain and grief for many years," Kerm added.

"It is not easy for me." Darrogh clenched his hands into fists. "Until I joined Ardal's unit, I had never been near women."

Breanon paused in cleaning his rifle. "You must have had some contact."

Darrogh shook his head. Only Ardal, their leader, knew of his previous military deployments. The other men in the unit had accepted that Darrogh had earned his position as second in command. They had never inquired about his experiences before he had joined their unit.

"I was trained and fought on Cosnov. We did not have women there."

"It was known as the death planet." Breanon frowned. "It would have been severe."

"Very few of the Hunters in my division survived."

A Hunter's purpose was to fight. Death was expected, and to die in battle was an honor. He had lived. Most of those he had fought with, had died. He didn't question why. He knew that his years of battle had made him a superior warrior. Now, for the first time, he realized that those skills could be used for something he cared about. Protecting Tamsin.

"I battled in the frontlines of many wars until I was transferred to Thars Station. From there, I went to Ardal's unit. I was transferred one week before the Holman took over Cygnus."

Thars Station was a prison planet; brutal and primitive. Darrogh had been in charge of security and prisoner containment. The main activity there had been the mining and processing of Monazite, with most of its minerals being used for nuclear energy and weapons. It was a harsh environment. Prisoners worked with compliance or they were killed. There were no second chances.

"Guarding the High Council would have been a drastic change." Savis sat back from his computer. "You did not have time to adjust."

Darrogh clenched his jaw. "I arrived and immediately we were helping the council escape from the Holman. Because of my battle experience, I was left on Cygnus to defend the Council Chambers until everyone was safely off the planet."

Darrogh did not elaborate on the torture that had followed once the Holman had discovered that the Kaladin High Council had escaped. He was a Hunter. It was understood that he and his men had defended and delayed the enemy until they had been ordered to surrender as a delaying tactic. The Holman might have thought that they could break him, but they were wrong. When Ardal and the rest of the unit had returned, that was when they had been shipped off for execution.

"I can understand your concern about women and this planet," Kerm said. "It is not for us to question the pair bond. It is a part of being a Hunter and you would be foolish to ignore it."

"I had not considered that." Darrogh paused as he reflected on this new perspective. "To be a Hunter also means the possibility of a pair bond."

"It has made Ardal a better leader," Savis said.

"It is who we are." Breanon clicked the magazine back into his rifle. "We protect and obey women. Now we know we can also form a pair bond and mate."

"It's part of our breeding." Kerm spoke in a firm voice. "If we hadn't been given implants at birth, we would not doubt it."

"We would have accepted bonding along with all of our other modifications." Savis glanced down at his computer.

"You are right," Darrogh agreed.

A weight had been lifted from him. He had never considered that bonding was an extension of being a Hunter, and therefore as natural as their duty to fight and die. There was no dishonor in accepting Tamsin as his pair bond. The ability to form a bond with a woman and mate had been a part of him since birth. It had nothing to do with Earth. The Kaladin had denied him that right by using implants. He was now free of those restraints.

"I will advise the others of what has happened to me."

Darrogh had wasted enough time with doubt and questions.

He brought his focus back to the mission.

"Peter is bouncing up and down." Savis spoke in a hesitant voice. "I do not know if that means he has spotted someone or wants our help."

"Has he said anything?"

"No." Savis looked up at Darrogh. "His microphone is working because I can hear the sound of the water in the fountain."

"Is that masking his words?"

"I am uncertain." Savis leaned closer to his monitor. "His camera is pointing toward a dark figure that is standing by the trees."

"Tell me when it moves." Darrogh eased the tension from his shoulders. "It may be his contact and they are making certain that Peter is alone."

Years of battle had taught Darrogh patience. It was better to wait for the enemy to come to him, then to be on the offensive. If this was Peter's client, then they would know soon enough who their enemy was. The threat against Tamsin could only be defeated once they knew the exact nature of what they were dealing with.

"The figure is moving toward Peter." Savis's voice broke the silence.

"Good." Darrogh walked to the computer. "It is still too dark to make out the man's face."

The person moved closer. Lamplight lit the features enough that they knew they were dealing with a man. He was dressed in a dark overcoat and had a woolen cap on his head. It would make identification difficult if he stayed at a distance.

"Breanon you are the only one of us who has not been seen guarding Tamsin. Get ready to follow in case we cannot get a visual on the client."

Breanon put his rifle down and stood at the door.

Just then, the man came within camera view.

His face was clear and there was no mistaking his identity. The man who had hired Peter to follow and photograph Tamsin was her father's assistant, Henry Kingsley.

Chapter 15

"Why would he want Tamsin followed?" Savis adjusted the sound on the computer speakers.

Peter's voice could be heard. "You got my note."

"This had better be good. It's dangerous to meet." Henry's voice was clear.

"I don't have any more photos. My cover was blown."

"You dragged me here for that." Henry's voice was a low growl.

"Those bodyguards are Hunters. You should have told me that." Peter's voice sounded irritated. "It only took them a week to discover I was following her. They grabbed my camera and destroyed it."

"You're off the job."

"No kidding." Peter's voice rose. "I want money for my equipment. We agreed to expenses."

"I don't want to see you again." Henry shoved a bundle of bills at Peter. "Forget that we ever did business if you want to live."

"Easily." Peter pushed the bills into his upper pocket, sending the camera careening off to the side. "I'm going to give you some friendly advice. Don't fool around with those guys. They'll rip you apart."

"They're no match for the people I work with." Henry's tone was boastful.

"You do know what Hunters are?" Peter asked. "They follow a code and if you harm Tamsin Creighton, they'll kill you."

"They can try." Henry gave a low chuckle. "They won't know where the attack comes from."

Peter shrugged. "It's your funeral. I've done my part and warned you."

Henry walked away. Within seconds, he'd faded into the background of the muted lighting of the park. Darrogh motioned to Breanon, who left the van to follow. They needed to see if he met anyone.

Kerm started the van. He had shifted the vehicle into gear and was about to drive away when a sharp knock at the side stopped him.

"Let me in." Peter banged the van again.

Darrogh nodded. When the photographer was inside they drove off in the direction that Kingsley had taken.

"*He's crossed Park Lane and is entering Grosvenor House.*" Breanon reported through mind connection.

"Grosvenor House." Darrogh told Kerm.

"How can you possibly know that?" Peter's voice was suspicious.

Darrogh turned back to the man. "If you continue to interfere, we will drop you off here."

Peter put up his hand. "I'll be quiet."

"Give me the camera you are wearing." Darrogh held his hand out to Peter.

Peter raised an eyebrow, but unclipped it from his collar and handed it over.

"*Breanon, meet me at the Grosvenor entrance.*" Darrogh issued his order through mind connect.

"Kerm keep driving around the block." Darrogh stood and gripped the handle of the side door. "I will meet up with you."

When the van was in front of the luxury hotel, he opened the door and jumped out. Breanon was standing at the side of the Ballroom entrance. Darrogh ran to him and passed him the small camera.

"Keep as close as possible without being seen."

Breanon nodded and walked to the hotel's entrance.

Darrogh went in the opposite direction. About five minutes later, he saw the van turning the block. He jogged over, and when the side door opened, he jumped in. Peter was shaking his head at him when he landed with a thud on the metal of the vehicle floor. The door was slammed shut and they continued to drive around the block.

"You guys are crazy." Peter crossed his arms and leaned back in his seat.

Darrogh ignored the comment and turned to Savis. "Has Breanon found him?"

"Kingsley is seated in the lobby. Breanon has him in his sights."

"Good." Darrogh stood.

Darrogh watched the computer screen. Kingsley was sitting in a luxurious leather seat in the main reception area. He was tapping a foot, and every few seconds, he would swing his head around as if he were looking for someone. It took another five minutes before there was any change in his behavior. His head turned at the opening of the elevator doors. He stood and straightened his jacket before walking over to the elevator.

Three men dressed in long black coats exited the lift.

Albireons.

Darrogh had seen enough. He could not risk putting Breanon in any more danger. The Albireons were unaware that Darrogh and his men knew about them, and he wanted it to remain that way as long as possible. For now, it was enough to know where the leak was in Creighton's.

"*Return.*" He relayed the order to Breanon.

"Make certain we have a copy of this. Sir Robert will want evidence." Darrogh straightened away from the computer. "Send it through to Ardal. He needs to know how far-reaching the infiltration is."

The van continued to circle the block until Breanon was within sight. Once the last team member was onboard, they left the area for Tamsin's house. The sooner they were able to delve into this new evidence, the better.

Darrogh's anxiety over Tamsin's safety was increasing. Knowing that the Albireons were directly involved in threatening her had heightened his concern. Worse, they had been doing it for months, and the degree of their infiltration into Creighton's, was chilling. This menace must be dealt with. He would not rest until Tamsin was safe.

"Are you guys going to tell me what's happening?" Peter asked.

Darrogh had forgotten about the photographer in his hurry to return to Tamsin. "We will take you home."

"No. I go with you." Peter rubbed his arms. "Whatever has you moving so fast, is something I need to be afraid of. You're not keeping me out of the loop now."

Darrogh considered the human for a second. He was unkempt and irritating, yet he had managed to elude their surveillance for almost a week. He was observant and quick to understand a situation. He might be useful as long as he could be trusted.

"If Kingsley or the Albireons discover that Peter is working with us, then his life is in danger too." Savis's voice was matter of fact. "We need to protect him."

"If you stay, you must understand that we will not tolerate any betrayal." Darrogh's voice was stern. "I will do my best to ensure your safety, but I cannot guarantee it. The penalty for deceiving us is death."

Peter's eyes widened. "You're serious."

Darrogh crossed his arms. "Do you want us to take you home?"

Peter shook his head. "I'm a good investigator. You guys need me."

"We will discuss strategy when we are in a secure area."

They reached Tamsin's house on Chelsea Square less than fifteen minutes later. They parked the van in the street behind and then took the rear entrance into the house. When they entered the kitchen, Firbin was waiting.

"Jehon is in the lounge with Tamsin."

"Make certain everything is secure and then meet us there."

Darrogh moved through the house to the front reception rooms. The other men followed. When they entered the lounge, Tamsin stood. She was the most beautiful woman he had ever seen and seeing her released the knot of tension in his chest. A surge of relief flowed through Darrogh.

She was safe.

"What's happened?" Tamsin made a move toward him and then stopped herself.

"We have evidence of who has been following you." Darrogh nodded toward Peter. "Henry Kingsley is Peter's client."

Tamsin sank back into her chair. "How could he?"

Savis brought the computer over to her and showed the video they had filmed.

"My father has to be told." Tamsin looked up from the monitor.

"We will make him aware." Darrogh crossed his arms. "There is something else."

"What?"

"Kingsley met up with Albireons."

Tamsin frowned. "So he's working with Albirsion Corporation."

Savis keyed in the video that Breanon had taken. Tamsin's eyes narrowed as she watched Kingsley meet up with the three men dressed in black. The video followed the men until they turned toward the lobby. The last image that Breanon had captured was the faces of the men dressed in black overcoats with their sunglasses and fedora hats. The video was frozen on their eerie faces.

"Who are they?" Peter leaned closer to the screen. "Their faces don't look right."

"That's because they're not human. They come from another planet." Darrogh walked to the computer and pointed his finger at the three figures on the monitor. "They are Albireons."

Peter started to laugh. "That's a great joke. Aliens."

"I think the hats and sunglasses make them look almost human." Tamsin's tone was musing. "I would never have given them a second look if I'd seen them on the street. Are they really behind the threats to my father's bank?"

"Worse." Savis closed the video. "One of our brothers escaped their clutches in Australia. His mate was being restrained and ready to be experimented on when he rescued her."

A shiver went through Tamsin. "How horrible."

"You guys are serious." Peter's mouth dropped open as he looked at each of them. "There is no such thing as extra-terrestrials."

"Believe what you want." Darrogh crossed his arms over his chest. "Albireons, like Hunters, are not from Earth."

Peter's eyes narrowed. "Are you saying what I think you are?"

"If you are working with us, you need to understand what we are fighting."

"You look human." Peter's voice faded away.

"We are genetically human, but we originated on a different planet." Savis's voice was matter of fact. "Our genes have been modified."

"That's not possible." Peter shook his head.

"Enough debate. We need to eliminate this threat." Darrogh's voice was stern. There was no time to waste if they were going to keep Tamsin alive. "With Henry Kingsley working for the Albireons, the bank has been compromised. Savis can you determine how deep the infiltration is?"

"I will need access to their computer systems."

Darrogh looked at Tamsin. Disbelief and shock were written all over her face. The situation was serious and he did not have the time to let her process Kingsley's betrayal. He sent her a wave of calm and then strength. If there was any hope of stopping the Albireons, they had to act fast.

"Can you get access Tamsin?"

She looked up at him. "I don't work there anymore."

"We will have to tell your father."

"It will kill him." Tamsin's voice was hushed. "He thinks of Henry like a son."

"Losing you would be much worse." Darrogh did not try to soften his words. He needed to say something that would shock her out of her stupor. It took a second, but she straightened her shoulders.

"You're right." Tamsin looked at Savis. "Is tomorrow soon enough?"

Savis nodded. "I will see what I can do from here tonight."

"Rest first." Darrogh's voice was a command. "Now that we know the level of our threat, we will double our watches. Breanon and I will take the first shift."

Breanon nodded and left the room. Darrogh went to the windows and rechecked their locks before closing the curtains. His men needed sleep. It was unlikely that the Albireons would strike immediately. The news that their surveillance on Tamsin had been stopped would take them a while to process. Albireons were notoriously slow at reacting to new situations. In the past, Darrogh had used that to his advantage to defeat them. Tonight might be their only reprieve, so he wanted everyone well-rested before they battled the enemy.

"What about me?" Peter's voice was a low whine.

"You wanted to come with us." Darrogh's voice was harsh. "Your skills will be needed."

Peter straightened his shoulders. "I understand, but I need to sleep."

Tamsin stood. "You can have the den. It has a comfortable couch. The rest of the rooms are being used by the men."

When Tamsin and Peter had left, Firbin looked at him. "Was it wise to tell the human?"

"We had no choice." Darrogh pushed away his own doubts. "His services might be useful and I think once he has processed everything, he will be fine."

"We still have his photos." Savis stood. "In the morning I will have him re-examine everything to see if there is a pattern. We may be able to find out where the Albireons have stationed themselves."

"Look into Grosvenor House." Darrogh leaned against the fireplace. "If there is a nest of them there, we will eliminate it first."

Savis picked up his computer. "I will access their files."

"Work begins in the morning," Darrogh said. "We need to understand the full extent of the Albireon infiltration into the bank before we can act. I will apprise Ardal of the situation in case we need reinforcements."

The men left the room.

Darrogh wiped a hand over his face. The threat to Tamsin was worse than he had originally suspected. It was one thing to think that humans might be out to hurt her, but to know that it was Albireons, heightened his concern. He had always been vigilant when on a protection mission, but this was the first time he was personally involved in the outcome.

"You look deep in thought." A surge of joy raced through him at the sound of Tamsin's voice. "Are these aliens that big of a threat?"

"They can be defeated."

"That's not reassuring." Tamsin sat on the sofa. "You sound as if you're planning a battle."

"I am." Darrogh sat beside her. "Why is it necessary to control your father's bank? Albirsion Corporation already owns over fifty banks world-wide."

"The more banks you have, the greater your power?" Tamsin shrugged her shoulders.

"Is there something special about Creighton's bank?"

"Creighton's holds the money of many of the world's richest families. We have always been the bank of choice for those with wealth. Our reputation has been built on service and discretion."

"Controlling Creighton's gives them a position of power over those who have influence." Darrogh was beginning to understand the necessity of keeping Creighton's free from the Albireons. "If they are targeting your father's bank, they do not yet have control of the wealthiest people on this planet."

"It would make sense." Tamsin clasped his hand. "If they have that much power are you going to be able to keep us safe?"

"Always."

Darrogh looked down at their joined hands. A sense of peace and purpose filled him. It was right that he was here with Tamsin. He raised her hand to his lips and kissed it.

"I told you I was uncertain of the attraction between us." Darrogh's voice was hoarse. "I have no doubts now."

"You have decided it is too great a risk." Tamsin's voice sounded resigned.

"Never." Darrogh lifted her chin so that their eyes met. "You are my pair bond. It does not matter if you accept the connection because I know it to be true."

"You had doubts earlier. What changed?"

"I realized that my feelings and bonding had nothing to do with this planet." Darrogh's voice was serious. "I am a Hunter and we form pair bonds with one woman only. That is part of our breeding. Implants were the only reason that it had not happened in the past. Being on Earth has nothing to do with our ability to find a mate."

"So what does that mean for us?"

"I trust who I am as a warrior and as a Hunter." Darrogh's words were like a vow. "I am bonded to you and I will always be with you. You are a part of me. Your wishes are my desires."

Tamsin's eyes filled with tears. "I still don't know if I believe what is happening between us."

Darrogh wiped away one of Tamsin's tears with his thumb. "I am completely committed and bound to you. Nothing can change that. I will protect and defend you with my last dying breath."

Darrogh gathered her close.

He sensed her indecision.

It did not change how he felt. She was in danger and for the first time he realized that his years of fighting and battle had prepared him for this moment. Tamsin needed his protection and skills. He would defend her to the death and beyond.

Chapter 16

Tamsin woke up refreshed. She couldn't remember feeling this good since before her mother had died when she was ten years old. That seemed a lifetime ago. She sat up in bed and stretched her arms over her head. That's when she saw him.

Darrogh.

The man who claimed her as his pair bond.

She wasn't exactly certain what that meant, but she knew she'd never felt this way about any other man. It was terrifying and glorious at the same time. He sensed her thoughts and if he was telling the truth, she would be able feel his also. Right now, all she had to do was look at him to know what he was thinking.

Tenderness and concern shone from his eyes.

A fierce protectiveness underlined his whole being. It was in his stance and the way he moved. This man was definitely the warrior he claimed to be, and he had vowed to keep her safe. With him beside her, she knew there would never be any need for concern. It was a shock to realize that she didn't question this knowledge.

The first glimmer of belief was seeping through her doubts.

Trust would follow.

"Did you stay awake all night?" Tamsin hugged her knees under the bed covers.

"Firbin and Savis took a shift." Darrogh's voice was low. "I just came in a few minutes ago."

"Have you had breakfast yet?"

"We have fed ourselves." Darrogh leaned forward in the floral armchair he was sitting in. "Are you ready to start the day? We have a lot to accomplish and time is important."

"You mean the Albireons will be after us shortly."

"They will try." Darrogh's eyes narrowed. "They do not move as quickly as other races. They are slow and methodical. It will take them a few days to process what has happened and that will give us the time we need to defeat them."

"You've done this before." Tamsin had a brief flash of light and explosions. Intuitively, she knew that she was seeing something that had happened to Darrogh in the past.

"I have fought many a battle with this enemy." Darrogh nodded. "My experience will be useful for this fight."

A shiver raced through her. The thought of blood being shed and people dying because of the need to protect a bank was repulsive. She valued life too much to believe that any good could come from open warfare. She would never forgive herself if others had to die to protect Creighton's.

"I am guarding you, not a bank." Darrogh's words brought her focus back to him. "Protecting Creighton's bank from Albireon control means that we are stopping the complete annihilation of this planet. Many lives will the saved."

Tamsin nodded. "I hadn't considered that."

"There would be no honor in endangering people needlessly." Darrogh's voice was matter of fact.

"I'm learning to trust you." Tamsin smiled and leaned back against the cushioned headboard of her bed. "You live by honor and truth."

"And the Sacred Code." Darrogh's gaze softened. "To know that my skill and training are being used to protect you has given me a true purpose in life."

A warm glow filled Tamsin. There was silence for several seconds as they gazed at each other. She was drowning in his eyes and only the rumbling of her stomach brought her back to the present. They had real enemies to defeat, and the sooner they started, the better.

"I need coffee and then I'll be ready to face the day."

Darrogh stood.

At that moment, the door burst open, and her father rushed in shaking a newspaper in the air. "What the hell were you thinking?"

Darrogh reacted faster than she'd ever seen a person do before. He reached her father and pushed him back against the wall before she could blink. Her eyes widened as she watched her father struggle against Darrogh's grip on his coat lapels. Darrogh raised him from the floor.

"Put me down." Her father's words came out in a burst of rage. "I'm her father. I have every right to see her."

"No one speaks or approaches Tamsin in anger." Darrogh's voice came through clenched teeth. "It does not matter who you are."

"It's fine Darrogh." Tamsin motioned to put her father down. "My father would never harm me."

Darrogh let her father slip down the wall. He stepped back and shut the door. "I will not leave you here with her alone."

"This concerns both of you." Robert Creighton straightened his shirt and jacket. "Have you seen the morning papers?"

"I just woke up." Tamsin reached for the paper that her father threw at her.

She took one look and her stomach dropped.

Plastered on the front page, was the photo that Peter had taken of Darrogh carrying her in his arms. Below that, was a picture of her getting into Saxby's car. The headlines read 'Banker's Daughter Caught in Drunken Orgy'. There was no hiding the fact that she'd been with Saxby. The evidence was there for all the world to see.

She handed the paper to Darrogh.

His eyes narrowed. "Now we know what happened to the photos."

Tamsin sighed. It was too early in the morning for this. She needed a coffee and a few minutes to consider what this would mean, not only for her, but for Creighton's Bank. If they were trying to undermine the bank's reputation by smearing her name, they were doing a good job of it.

"What pictures?" Robert Creighton looked at her and she shrugged.

"I've been followed by a detective for months now."

"We caught him yesterday." Darrogh tossed the newspaper on the bed. "We knew about the photos and we found out who his client was."

"I should have been told immediately." Robert Creighton pointed his finger at Darrogh. "You answer to me."

Darrogh shook his head. "I protect Tamsin and that means I do what is best for her safety."

Robert Creighton swatted the paper against his hand. "It looks like you're doing more than that. I hired you to guard my daughter, nothing more."

Darrogh's chin jutted out and for a second Tamsin thought that he was going to react to her father's taunt. Instead, he took a step back. He crossed his arms over his chest and looked at her. She could have sworn she heard his voice asking what she wanted. Despite the differences she had with her father and his efforts to control her life, she loved and trusted him. He needed to be told the truth.

"Sit down, Dad." Tamsin motioned her father to the chair that Darrogh had vacated. "A lot has happened since Saturday night."

"The whole world knows that, thanks to those pictures." Robert Creighton sat. "Why didn't you tell me about this sooner?"

"We just found out yesterday." Tamsin glanced at Darrogh. "Could you get us some coffee?"

Darrogh looked at her with a stubborn intensity.

"He needs to hear this from me."

She sent the message to Darrogh through her mind. If he could truly connect to her, he would hear her words and understand.

"Your daughter's safety is the only thing I care about." Darrogh's voice was low. "If you endanger her in any way, you will answer to me."

He left the room.

She released the breath she'd been holding. Darrogh had told her the truth when he'd said they were connected on more than one level.

"I'm waiting." Her father's voice dragged her back to the room.

"I wish you had told me why you had hired bodyguards for me in the beginning. It would have made things easier."

"I'm your father and I was protecting you." Her father's voice was sharp. "I don't have to explain all of my actions to you."

"When they involve me, you do." Tamsin kept her voice low. "I'm an adult now and capable of making my own decisions."

"Like you did with Winchester and the wedding."

Tamsin nodded. "Exactly like that. I knew I couldn't marry him, but I went along with it because you wanted the union. When I found him in bed with Liz that was the last straw. I didn't care what it took, I was going to cut my ties with him, and you, if necessary. I wasn't going to be married to a man who didn't love me."

"Is love what you think you've found with Darrogh?" Robert Creighton's words sounded more like an insult than a question.

Tamsin took a deep breath. "I don't understand what is happening between Darrogh and myself. I do know he doesn't lie to me, he's saved my life, and he will continue to protect me no matter what I do."

"He's a bodyguard for God's sake. He's beneath you in class and education."

Tamsin couldn't believe her father's prejudice. "I'm not prepared to discuss him with you. Do you want to know what happened on the night these photos were taken?"

Her father crossed his arms and looked away for a few seconds before turning back to her. It was a tactic he'd used since she was a child whenever he'd been displeased with her behavior. The familiar knot in her stomach tightened before a sense of calm came over her. She couldn't be certain, but it felt as if Darrogh was reaching out to her.

"Tell me," her father ordered.

"I resented you hiring men to guard me. I thought it was another trick you were using to get me under your control again, so I did everything in my power to escape. Saturday night was the first time I succeeded."

"So you went to a party where you got drunk?" Her father shook his head. "You've just proved my point that you need looking after."

"I wasn't drunk in that photo." Tamsin paused for a second. "I'd been drugged with Rohypnol. If Darrogh hadn't arrived when he did, I would have been raped and murdered."

Her father's eyes widened. "How could you let yourself get into that situation?"

"I met someone that I had gone to school with and he agreed to help me evade my bodyguards. I thought I was safe with George Saxby, so I pretended to go to the Ladies Room and then ducked out the fire exit."

"Where were your bodyguards?"

"Luckily, they weren't far behind." Tamsin pushed past her reluctance to remember what had happened that night. "George said that he would drive me home. After I got in his car, he insisted on going back to his place for a drink."

"You know better than that." Her father's criticism stabbed like a dagger.

"I went to university with him. How was I to know he'd become a predator?" Tamsin lifted her chin. "I was desperate to get away from the men that I thought were spying on me. I took a chance."

"What happened next?"

"I took a couple of sips of wine and then I couldn't move." Tamsin blinked back her tears. Images from that night were still coming back in pieces. The horror, and fear were still with her.

"George hit me and ripped my clothes, and when I threatened to tell the police, he swore he would kill me." Tamsin's voice shook. "That's when I realized what a fool I'd been to leave the protection of Darrogh and his men."

"It was a little late by then." Creighton's voice cracked. "How did you escape?"

"I swore I heard Darrogh's voice in my head telling me everything would be okay and then they rescued me." Tamsin wiped the tears from her cheek. "That picture was taken after they had made certain George would never hurt another woman."

"You're okay?" Her father reached over and clasped her hand. "Thank God the men arrived in time. I couldn't have handle it if that monster had killed you."

There was a knock at the door and then Darrogh came in with two mugs of coffee. He handed her one and then went to her father. Robert Creighton's hand was shaking as he took the cup from Darrogh. The two men looked at each other for a second and then Darrogh closed the door and leaned against it with his arms crossed. Relief flooded her. She needed Darrogh's support for the rest of the interview with her father.

Robert Creighton took several sips of his coffee before he looked at Darrogh. "What did you do to Saxby?"

"He is dead." Darrogh's voice held no emotion. "He pulled a gun on me and we wrestled with it. I made certain he was shot in the head."

"So it was self-defense." Her father's voice held relief. "There will be no legal ramifications."

"He had broken the code all Hunters live by and death was the only choice for him. He knew I was going to kill him for harming Tamsin."

Her father's mouth dropped open. "You can't go around killing people. I don't need the kind of publicity a trial would bring. I asked you to keep my daughter safe, nothing more."

"Honor and justice demanded that George Saxby die." Darrogh's voice was firm. "Tamsin was not the first women to be hurt by that man."

Sir Robert exhaled. "Even though I would have liked to kill him with my bare hands for touching Tamsin, I would have let the law deal with it."

"They would not have brought justice or closure to those he harmed. His death will do that."

Her father turned away from Darrogh and looked at her with a stunned expression. "Do you condone what they did?"

"He caused his own death in this case." A chill rushed through Tamsin. "He would have killed me if they hadn't stopped him."

"I understand." Her father's voice was filled with empathy. "That is why we have the police and laws, though."

"I wasn't in any state to think." Tamsin's voice trembled. "I couldn't move. Darrogh carried me out of the building and that's when the picture was taken."

Her father stood and picked up the paper. "All you can see is a brick wall in the background. Nobody should be able to connect you with Saxby's death."

"We cleaned up all evidence of Tamsin," Darrogh said. "This is not our first time circumventing the law."

A vein bulged in her father's neck. "I appreciate and thank you for saving my daughter's life. I can't condone you killing people, though. If you can't follow the law, I'll have no choice but to fire you."

Chapter 17

"I vowed to protect Tamsin." Darrogh kept his voice calm. "I am not leaving."

"I'd be an accomplice if I allowed you to kill people." Tamsin's father's face was twisted with anger. "It'll look worse because I pay you. That makes it murder for hire."

"We do not need money to do what is right."

Darrogh walked over to Tamsin. He sensed her frustration and disappointment at her father's reaction to her ordeal. A part of him wished to order the man out of the house, but they needed his help with the Albireons. It would be easier to gain access to the bank's computers if Sir Robert sanctioned it.

"Tamsin was almost killed by that monster. She still has the bruises from his attack." Darrogh's hands clenched into fists. The faint discoloration on Tamsin's cheek was a reminder of his failure to protect her. "She needs your love and support."

Robert Creighton looked over at his daughter. "Are you certain you want these men protecting you?"

"They're the only ones keeping me safe." Tamsin's voice shook. "Please listen, Dad. Something else has happened."

Creighton sighed. He glanced up at Darrogh before looking back at Tamsin. "You have ten minutes to explain."

"Let me get dressed." Tamsin pushed back her bed covers. "I'll meet you downstairs in the lounge."

Darrogh opened the door and waited for Sir Robert to leave before closing it. "Do you need me to stay?"

Tamsin shook her head. "Give me a few minutes and I'll be downstairs."

Darrogh sent her a surge of calming energy before leaving the room. When he reached the first floor, Sir Robert was pacing in the lounge. Darrogh went to the fireplace and crossed his arms. He motioned to Savis.

"Show Sir Robert the photos of Tamsin."

Savis had been working on his laptop at a desk in the corner. When Creighton sat beside him, he started to scroll through the photographer's pictures. It took several minutes. Tamsin had joined them by the time they were finished.

She was wearing black pants and a bright, floral silk blouse with a matching jacket. Darrogh's breath caught in his throat when she entered the room. She gave him a smile that sent his heart rate soaring before she sat on the sofa.

"This man has been following you for months." Creighton looked up from the computer screen. "Why didn't we see him earlier?"

"Because I'm good." Peter's voice rang out from the doorway. He was standing there with a cup of coffee and a grin on his face. "You should be thankful I'm part of your security team now."

"I hired him," Tamsin added.

"Without my permission?" Her father leaned back in his chair and looked at Tamsin. "You can't be serious."

"You need me." Peter took a sip of coffee and sat on the edge of the desk beside Savis and Sir Robert. "I'm the one who took the photos that the newspaper printed."

"My daughter doesn't need a paparazzo."

"I'm a private investigator." Peter's voice was defensive. "I handed those photos over to my client. He's the one who sold them to the papers."

"Who is your client?" Sir Robert spoke through gritted teeth.

"We set up a meeting last night and followed Peter." Darrogh nodded to Savis who pulled up their surveillance from the previous night.

Creighton jumped back when he saw Henry Kingsley. His eyes widened as he watched the slide show of photos on the screen. When it was over, he sat back.

"I don't understand. Why was Henry there?"

"He was my client." Peter pointed to the last picture of Kingsley meeting with the Albireons. "It looks like he's working with these guys."

"Who are they?" Sir Robert looked up at Darrogh.

"They are Albireons." Darrogh walked over to Tamsin and stood behind her. "If you searched Peter's photos from the past few months, you would have seen similar men following her."

"Are these the people threatening my daughter?" Creighton's voice rose. "You have the evidence. Call the police and charge them with stalking."

"It's a bigger problem than you understand, Dad." Tamsin's voice was calm. "These aren't normal men."

"Supposedly, they are extra-terrestrials." Peter's voice held a hint of laughter. "And apparently these men you hired to protect your daughter, are also aliens."

Creighton's eyes bulged. "Is everyone here crazy?"

Darrogh was about to speak when Tamsin put up her hand. "This is not a laughing matter. You need to listen. Darrogh and his men have dealt with these people before."

"Don't tell me you're buying all this alien stuff?" Creighton's voice was accusing as he turned to his daughter.

Tamsin hesitated a few seconds before nodding her head. "I believe them. I think you should too."

Creighton gave his daughter a long considering look and then took a deep breath. He turned to Darrogh. "Explain."

"We have encountered this race in Australia." Darrogh's voice was low. "They are partnered with a covert agency that does not have ties to any country. They are experimenting on humans."

"Do you have proof?" Peter's voice was filled with doubt. "People go around saying they've seen aliens, but when it comes down to it, there's no evidence."

"That's because there are humans who are working with the Albireons."

"I need a photograph or something more concrete." Peter took a sip of coffee. "Hearsay won't do."

"The mate of one of our warriors was captured. She had been in the FBI." Darrogh kept his impatience under control. He knew it was difficult for humans to believe that life existed on other planets. "She was close enough to the Albireons to see that they were not from Earth."

Peter shook his head. "Anybody can say that."

"The photographs show the truth. The men are not human." Savis magnified one of the Albireons from Henry Kingsley's meeting. "Take a close look at their faces. There are no eyebrows, facial hair or lips."

Peter and Robert Creighton moved closer to the screen. They watched as Savis enlarged a number of the images from the previous night. Savis also went through some of the photos of the men who had followed Tamsin over the past month. They all showed the same defects; no facial hair, a slit for a mouth, and pale pasty-colored skin. They wore the same uniform of a dark overcoat, black pants, and a black fedora hat.

"It's impossible to believe that there would be so many men with the same defects." Robert Creighton leaned back. "You believe that they're extra-terrestrials?"

"I know they are." Darrogh pulled his shirt out of his pants and turned so his back was exposed. "These scars came from the Boglara Frontier. I was captured by Albireons and before I could escape, they had taken slices of me for their experiments and genetic database."

Tamsin inhaled a sharp breath. "Your back is a mass of scars."

Darrogh let his shirt drop. "I was lucky. I freed myself and then killed my captors. I know first-hand the damage that Albireons can do. On the Boglara Frontier, they had conquered and decimated several planets before we defeated them."

"Why are they on Earth?" There was a tremor of shock in Creighton's voice.

"It is the same wherever they go. They gather all of the genetic material, strip the planet of its resources, and then destroy it. They leave with everything necessary to carry on their business."

"You mean it's a matter of economics?" Peter's tone held disbelief. "That seems extreme. What business are they in?"

"Genetic recombination for the purpose of selling slaves and new species." Savis shut his laptop. "They destroy all of the living components of a planet so that they hold the only copies of the genetic code."

"They mine our genes?" Creighton's voice rose in outrage. "How could humans possibly go along with this scheme?"

"The Albireons disguise their true purpose." Darrogh crossed his arms. "They promise wealth and knowledge in exchange for a chance to study a world. Over the years, they give away small amounts of technological information as they slowly infiltrate and take over the planet."

"So they hoodwink us."

Darrogh nodded. "They are masters of deception."

"There are very few galaxies that will allow them to do business," Savis added. "That is probably why they are on Earth. You are not advanced enough for extended space travel."

"How long have they been here?" There was a quiver in Tamsin's voice.

"Seventy or more years." Savis stood. "We are working on a way to defeat them. Right now there is a bigger problem."

"One that requires your help, Sir Robert."

Darrogh kept his voice unemotional. Creighton must understand the full extent of the Albireons' intrusion. Once they could manipulate the economics of Earth, they could start a world-wide panic that would result in them grabbing even more power.

"What can I possibly do?"

"We need access to your bank's computer records."

"Impossible."

"We believe that the Albireons have already infiltrated your bank." Darrogh straightened his shoulders. "They have been watching Tamsin for months, and they had an insider, Henry Kingsley, close to you. Who knows what damage has been done."

"Why Creighton's? Wouldn't the Central Bank make more sense?"

"They may already have that under their rule."

Darrogh looked at Tamsin's pale face and sent her a wave of strength. Neither she nor her father could imagine the extent of damage that the Albireons left in their wake. Darrogh never wanted them to experience that kind of devastation. It was imperative that they see the bank's files.

"Creighton's holds the money of many of the oldest and wealthiest families in the world. The Albireons could gain a lot of cooperation and power if they had these people in their control." Darrogh's explanation caught Creighton's attention.

"They want contact with my clients." Sir Robert nodded. "It makes sense. If what you say about Henry is true, and he has already given them access, how do you plan to remedy it?"

Darrogh looked at Savis.

"I have much experience with these systems," Savis said. "Once I know what has happened I will not only reverse it, but I will have a way to infiltrate their assets and holdings."

"You plan on taking everything they have." Creighton's voice was dry.

"It would be a mistake to do otherwise."

"We'll go to prison if we're caught." There were several minutes of silence while Sir Robert considered the proposition. He looked over at Tamsin. "Do you trust them?"

Darrogh's heart stopped for the few seconds it took Tamsin to answer.

She looked up at him and smiled.

"Yes." She turned to her father. "The Albireons have threatened us and Creighton's. It is our responsibility to stop them, no matter what."

"We've no choice but to take the offensive." Sir Robert heaved a sigh and stood. "Come around to the bank when you're ready and I'll give you the codes."

There was silence for several minutes after Sir Robert left the house.

"I never thought I'd find myself believing in aliens, but you guys are pretty convincing." Peter pushed away from the desk.

"Your photographs were the evidence." Savis put his computer into a slim bag that he threw over his shoulder. "The Albireons have had many years to do damage. It will take us a while to reverse it."

Tamsin stood. "I can help. I used to work at Creighton's. My father might find it easier if I asked all of the difficult questions."

"I am going with you." Darrogh's voice was sharp. "I will not risk your life."

Tamsin touched his hand. "I'll do what you want. We need to get busy on those files."

"Breanon you are to take point outside of the building. Firbin and Jehon will come with us."

"What about me?" Peter picked up his camera. "I can still shoot pictures of people coming and going."

Darrogh nodded. "Do not get in our way."

"Kerm will stay at the house. We cannot risk someone breaching security here."

"I'll get a jacket." Tamsin turned to go to her room, when she was stopped by the doorbell.

Darrogh stood in front of her and motioned for Kerm to answer it.

A minute later Kerm reported through mind connection. *"The police are here."*

Chapter 18

Tamsin was facing Darrogh's back.

When she tried to move around him, he stopped her. His arms blocked her on both sides. She'd never realized how large he was until this moment. Normally, she felt suffocated at being so close to a man, yet it was different with Darrogh. He made her feel safe and secure. She sensed that no matter what, he wouldn't allow anything to get by him.

"The police are here."

His words reverberated through her.

Her heart beat increased and she had to force herself to breathe. Why would they be here? The first thing that came to mind was Saturday night and what had happened at George's flat. So much had occurred since then that she'd completely blocked out the possibility of repercussions. Darrogh had assured her that there was no evidence of her at George's flat so it couldn't be about his death.

It must be something else.

Kerm led two women into the lounge. Tamsin had a quick glance of them before Darrogh blocked her view with his body. One was dressed in navy pants with a matching blazer. The outfit was a designer knock-off and suited her blonde hair and fair skin. The second woman, was attired more casually in a pair of black jean-styled pants and a floral blouse opened a few inches at the neckline. She had brown hair and sharp grey eyes. She looked at Darrogh.

"We're from the Metropolitan Police. I'm Detective Inspector Milton and this is Detective Sergeant Barlow. Is Miss Creighton here?"

Darrogh didn't move. "Why?"

"We have some questions about George Saxby," DS Barlow said.

"More specifically, about his death." DI Milton's tone was sharp.

Tamsin pushed at Darrogh's back. It was obvious that these women were not planning on leaving. For whatever reason, they thought that she had a connection with George. There was no point in avoiding their questions. They'd only come back later, or worse, haul her down to police headquarters.

"I didn't know he was dead. What do you want to know?" Tamsin's tone was hesitant as Darrogh stepped to the side.

DI Milton raised an eyebrow. "Are you expecting trouble in your own home?"

Tamsin gave Darrogh a quick glance. "He's one of my bodyguards. My father hired them because the bank has been receiving threats."

DI Milton looked at Darrogh and then glanced around the room at the other men. "You seem to have a lot of protection. Is there anything that the police should know about?"

Tamsin shook her head. "My father's overprotective."

DI Milton nodded. "When was the last time you saw George Saxby?"

Tamsin's mind froze. From the glance the two women sent her, she suspected a trap. They had seen the paper and probably already knew she'd been in his car recently. Her only course of action was honesty.

"Saturday night. I ran into George at Beauvie's." Tamsin forced her voice to remain casual. "We went to university together."

"So you were close friends." DS Barlow looked up from a notebook that she had been writing in.

"Not really." Tamsin swallowed to ease the dryness of her mouth.

"This is a picture of you getting into his car. What time was it?"

DI Milton pulled out a paper from the black tote bag she had over her shoulder. It was the same tabloid that her father had thrown at her this morning. The license of the vehicle was visible.

"Around midnight I think." Tamsin frowned. She honestly couldn't remember much of that night.

"Did he take you to his apartment?"

"Tamsin had nothing to do with this man's death." Darrogh voice boomed the denial.

DI Milton gave Darrogh a long look. "You knew she'd gone off with him."

"She was trying to avoid our protection." Darrogh's tone was cold. "Getting into this man's vehicle was not a wise decision."

DI Milton pointed at the second picture on the paper. The one where Darrogh was carrying her in his arms. "Where did you carry her from?"

"Is there a problem?"

"Just that Miss Creighton looks capable of walking when she got into the vehicle with George Saxby."

Darrogh straightened his shoulders. "Tamsin was tired when that picture was taken."

"I don't believe you." DI Milton's tone was sharp as she turned to Tamsin. "I think George Saxby drugged you, and made it impossible for you to move. That's why your bodyguard had to carry you. What else did he do?"

"Nothing." Tamsin forced outrage into her voice. "Why would you accuse George of such a thing?"

"Because that's what the man did." DS Barlow flipped through her notebook. "Apparently he made quite the hobby of drugging and raping women. The photos and videos left at his apartment even suggest that he might have murdered a few."

Tamsin inhaled a sharp breath. She'd known that George had intended to kill her, but she hadn't thought he'd murdered other women. "That's not the George I knew. How did he die?"

DS Barlow pointed her pen at Tamsin. "We found him shot with his own gun this morning and it looks like you may have been the last person to see him."

"That doesn't mean he drugged me."

"Did you go back to his flat?"

"Tamsin did nothing to this man." Darrogh took a step closer to her. "I can vouch for that."

"Where was this picture taken of you carrying her in your arms?" DI Milton's voice rose as she turned to interrogate Darrogh. "At his apartment?"

"At Beauvie's." Peter, who had been sitting on the couch spoke up. "Her bodyguard stopped the car and carried her away."

"Who are you?"

"I'm the guy who took the photographs." Peter cleared his throat. "I sold them to the tabloids. I didn't know what they had planned to do with them, so I came over to apologize."

DI Milton raised an eyebrow. "You'd be the first paparazzo to care about the effects your photos had."

Peter shrugged. "I'm actually a private investigator. I needed the money."

"And you're willing to swear that this photo of Miss Creighton in her bodyguard's arms was taken outside of Beauvie's?"

Peter nodded. "It's the truth."

"The brick in the picture looks similar to Saxby's building."

"All brick looks the same. I know where I took the photo." Peter leaned back on the couch. "Do you have any evidence that Miss Creighton was at this Saxby's apartment."

"No." DI Milton pursed her lips. "That doesn't prove anything. In my gut, I know she was involved."

"Everything was wiped clean from the surveillance video system he had at the building. It is all mysteriously blank. His computer is also missing." DS Barlow's voice was dry. "That in itself is suspicious."

"I wouldn't know the first thing about surveillance systems." Tamsin hugged herself to lessen her shaking.

These detectives were very close to discovering the truth, and she had the sickening feeling that Darrogh, if pressed, would admit to being there. The one thing she'd discovered since being protected by these men, was that they always told the truth when asked a direct question. It was fortunate that Peter had stepped in.

"I find it strange that you ran into your old friend on the same night he died."

"If he was killed with his own weapon could it not have been suicide?" Darrogh asked.

"We haven't ruled that out yet." DS Barlow shut her notepad.

"If you withhold any evidence from us, it will go against you if we find you're involved." DI Milton's voice was stern. "We're going to examine every camera from his building and the nightclub."

Darrogh nodded to Kerm. "Escort the detectives out."

When the detectives had left the room, Tamsin shoulders sagged. Her hands were shaking and she couldn't seem to focus on anything. Darrogh pulled her into his arms and held her until her trembling stopped. Then he led her to a chair so she could sit.

"Peter, why did you lie?" Tamsin's voice was a low whisper.

"It was obvious that you were going to try and brazen your way through the interview." Peter shrugged. "From the sounds of it, the man deserved to die."

"He pulled a gun on us and was shot in the struggle." Darrogh's voice was matter of fact. "I would have killed him, though. He broke the Sacred Code by doing harm to a woman. The penalty for that is death."

"Remind me not to get on your bad side." Peter shook his head. "If you're going to go around killing people, you have to take precautions."

"We did." Savis moved away from the desk he had been sitting at. "The police will find no evidence in the building, or on their CCTV cameras."

Peter's mouth dropped open. "You hacked their systems?"

"We swept the building and cameras clean. If we had known about your photographs, we would have stopped them from being published."

"Amazing." Peter rolled his eyes. "If there was a struggle and the gun went off, it was self-defense. You could have called the police. Instead, you've made yourselves look suspicious."

"We could not let Tamsin's abuse by that man be known," Darrogh said.

"Well it looks like you're in the clear." Peter stood. "I'm going to put my investigative skills to use today and follow Henry Kingsley."

"Is that wise?" Tamsin asked.

"I don't like being taken for a sucker." Peter grabbed his camera bag from the floor. "He may lead me to someone else who's involved with this organization. I'll report back at the end of the day."

Silence followed Peter's departure from the room.

Tamsin clasped her hands and looked up at the men. "I want to thank you for what you did to save me."

"It was our duty to keep you safe." Breanon's voice was low.

"I behaved badly." Tamsin cleared her throat. "I was angry with my father for insisting that you protect me, so I tried everything in my power to get away. It was foolish. Saxby intended to kill me. It was only your efforts that kept me alive."

Darrogh nodded. "It is an honor to give you protection. Now, we must find out the extent of damage done to your father's bank."

Tamsin sighed. "My father doesn't fully believe what you told him this morning about Henry working for the Albireons. You'll have to give him undeniable proof that Henry is working against Creighton's."

"Savis will find the evidence."

The men left the room, leaving her alone with Darrogh.

He held his hand out to her. She took it, almost reeling from the surge of sensation that raced up through her arm. She let him gather

her close. All the intrigue and stress of the past few days eased away. In its place, peace.

She looked up at Darrogh and smiled. He was the one who made everything right in her life. Even in the middle of being questioned by the police, and knowing that there were threats against her life, he'd been her anchor. She felt safe in his arms.

"Thank you." She brushed a hand down his cheek.

Darrogh leaned his forehead against hers. "I need to get you away from London soon. I cannot bear that your life is in danger here."

"Nothing can hurt me as long as you are with me." Tamsin pulled his head down to hers and moved her lips across his.

A sweet ache of need shot through her.

Darrogh deepened the kiss.

The world spun away. All that existed was her and Darrogh. She'd never known such a wonderful sensation of yearning and love mixed together. It was a connection that was spiritual and physical. Her body hummed with excitement.

All too soon, Darrogh ended the kiss.

"There is no doubt." His voice was hoarse. "You are my pair bond. I will never mate or desire another woman."

Tamsin longed to stay in his arms.

She'd been half a person until she'd met Darrogh.

Her whole life she'd searched for the unconditional love and devotion he offered. There would never be another man for her. It hit her with blinding clarity.

She was in love with Darrogh.

Chapter 19

Tamsin took a quick glance around the foyer of Creighton's Bank. Its familiarity had been a comfort to her when she was a child. She would come here with her father and visit with all of his employees. They treated her as if she were special and that had continued after she'd graduated and began to work here. This was the one place that had always felt like home to her.

That's why it had ripped her apart to leave the bank. Her father's insistence that she marry Winchester, despite his infidelity, had made it impossible for her to remain working here. She couldn't change the past, but she could make certain that her father's bank was safe. She was confident that Savis would find the information he needed.

"Miss Creighton." The bank's security guard, Smithson, stepped in front of her. "It's an age since you've visited."

She smiled at the older man. He'd been standing guard at the bank's entrance since before she was born. "Almost a year. How's your arthritis?"

"The doctor gave me some medicine to lessen the ache." Smithson grinned. "Sir Robert said to expect you this morning."

Tamsin heaved a sigh of relief. Her father had accepted the need to investigate the allegations against Henry. She turned to Savis and Darrogh.

"These are the men who will be accompanying me."

"Your father didn't mention anyone else." Smithson frowned. "I'll have to call him first."

Tamsin nodded. "We'll wait."

Darrogh leaned close and a shiver of awareness raced down her spine. "Is Sir Robert likely to deny us?"

"If he does, I'll speak with him." Tamsin fought the urge to lean against Darrogh. She straightened her shoulders and nodded at a few of the tellers who'd waved when they saw her.

"These people like you." Darrogh hadn't moved, yet it felt as if he'd reached out and embraced her with his whole being.

"I like them too." Tamsin kept her voice low. "When I was a child, this was my favorite place to visit. I loved it better than home."

"It must have been hard to leave."

"I couldn't continue working with my father."

A movement from above caught her attention.

Tamsin glanced at the large oak staircase that connected the main floor to the administrative section of the bank. Her father stood at the top. He looked as if he'd aged several years since this morning. Henry's betrayal had hit him hard.

Her father waved them up.

"Let me do the talking." Tamsin weaved her way through the customers and started up the stairs. "My father is a reasonable man, but sometimes, he needs time to process change."

"He has had enough." Savis's voice was dry. "His refusal to tell us the exact threat against you, has delayed us."

"True." Tamsin's voice was conciliatory. "He's my father, though. It can be challenging to deal with parents."

"We do not know about such things." Darrogh's voice was gruff.

Tamsin stopped walking and looked at the men. There was no sign of regret in either face, only acceptance. The loss of her mother had been devastating. As difficult as her father was, she couldn't have imagined a life without him.

"I'm sorry." Tamsin bit her lip. "I shouldn't have brought it up. I forgot."

"There is no need to apologize." Darrogh took her elbow and helped her up the first step. "Parents, and how to deal with them, has never been a problem for a Hunter."

Tamsin took a deep breath. These men may have come from a place that was technologically more advanced than Earth, but they'd missed a few things along the way. Who had guided them in their development?

"We were trained to be warriors from the day we could walk." Darrogh's voice was matter of fact. Again, he had read her thoughts, and was answering her question. "We did not have a childhood such as you do on Earth."

"That's terrible."

"It made us the best soldiers in the universe." Darrogh's voice held pride. "I am grateful. It means that I will be able to defend you no matter what happens."

Before Tamsin could reply, they had arrived at the top stair. Her father held his hand out to her. "I can take Tamsin from here."

Darrogh released her.

Loss of Darrogh's touch sent her reaching for him. His fingers brushed her arm, sending a shiver of awareness through her body. A sense of calm and peace came over her as her father pulled her away. She looked back at Darrogh. He followed and she had the distinct sensation that he was fighting the same need to connect as she was.

"I've set you up in your old office." Sir Robert's voice brought her back to the present. "I'll leave you alone once I've given you the access codes."

He opened the door to a large corner office. She walked in and gasped. Nothing had been changed since the day she'd left the bank. There was a black leather couch and a couple of chairs at one end, and her antique, library table that she used as a desk, at the other. Large windows on both walls framed her working space. She went to her desk and let her fingers brush over the battered oak surface.

"You kept it the same." Tamsin looked at her father. "Surely someone else needed the space."

"This has been your office since the day you entered the London School of Economics." Her father's voice held a note of pride. "As long as I'm running Creighton's, it will always be ready for you."

Tears pricked at her eyes. "Thank you."

She leaned over the desk and switched the computer on. While the computer was warming up, she motioned for Savis to sit. He put his own laptop beside the bank's monitor and started it up before looking at her father.

"I need complete access if I'm going to find out what has been happening."

Sir Robert pulled a sheet of paper out of his inside jacket pocket. "I'm the only one who has this level of clearance."

Savis reached for the codes. "It will only take a couple of hours. I will notify you with the results."

Sir Robert turned to Darrogh. "Where are your other men?"

"They are guarding Tamsin's house and the bank's exterior."

"You still think this is the work of a group of aliens bent on taking over the world?" Sir Robert shook his head. "I don't care how crazy you people are as long as I get results."

Darrogh inclined his head. "Our main concern is your daughter's safety. The only way we can secure that, is to stop what has been going on at this bank."

Sir Robert opened the door. "Let me know as soon as you find something concrete. I have no intention of confronting Henry with your slim allegations."

The door slammed on his exit.

Tamsin let out the breath she'd been holding. "I told you he could be difficult."

"We will find the evidence he requires." Darrogh's voice was firm as he leaned back against the office door. "After that, there will be no denying our words."

"Let's hope so."

Tamsin pulled up a chair beside Savis. For the next couple of hours, she watched as he ran various programs through the bank's records. Numbers flashed across the computer monitors with a blurring speed that had her head spinning. Every now and then, the screen would stop and Savis would frown, before he started up his scanning again.

Tamsin's back was aching and she stood to stretch. Darrogh was still on guard at the door. He'd barely moved since he'd taken up his position. It was amazing the stamina these men had. All she wanted to do was sink into one of her chairs and close her eyes. Looking at numbers flashing across a computer monitor was not her idea of fun.

"*Sit.*" Darrogh's words were a whisper in her mind. For a second she thought he'd said the word aloud. She looked at him and noticed the concern in his eyes.

She tried sending him a return thought. "*I'm fine.*"

Instantly, the anxiety left his eyes.

He'd heard her.

Tamsin's heart beat faster. She'd only half-believed Darrogh when he'd said that a pair bond could communicate with one another by thought. It was an experience she never believed possible. It was a total connection and oneness with each other. Before she had a chance to dwell on it further, Savis looked up from the computers.

"I've found the intrusion." His voice held a note of concern. "It is more complicated than we expected. It will take a while to devise a program to undo the damage."

"How severe is it?" Tamsin's didn't hide her anxiety.

"The majority of the bank's funds have been siphoned off to another location." Savis leaned back in his chair. "Your father needs to see the figures immediately so that we can take action."

Tamsin picked up the phone on her desk and punched in her father's extension. He answered after the first ring. "We've found the proof."

She hung up and waited. Sir Robert was outside the office within a couple of seconds. Darrogh let him in and then locked the door. He joined them at her desk.

"Show me." Her father's voice was hoarse with disbelief.

Savis brought up a number of columns and spreadsheets of figures. He scrolled through them until he reached the bottom. Her father frowned and then took the mouse from Savis. He scrolled up and then back to the bottom. When he was finished, he stood back and ran a hand over his face. When he looked at her, Tamsin thought he'd aged another ten years.

She urged him to sit. "Savis says that he can fix this."

"I can't believe it." Her father's voice was a low whisper. "I've thought of Henry like a son. There's no mistake. It's his access code that has been used to siphon all of the funds away from Creighton's. It was brilliant. We would never have found the breach until it was too late to do anything about it."

Savis pointed to the screen. "I've used his codes and transfer data to follow it through to its new home."

"Where does it go?" Tamsin looked back at the monitor.

"Two hundred thousand pounds went to Kingsley's personal account and the rest was moved to Nethercott Bank."

Tamsin opened her mouth to speak, and then shut it. Everything suddenly made sense. The rush for Winchester Nethercott to marry her and then merge with her father's bank. She'd thought Winchester's betrayal of her was bad enough, but what he'd done to her father and Creighton's, made her blood boil.

"There's no mistake?" Tamsin's voice cracked.

"Nethercott has the funds," Savis said. "Over eighty percent of Creighton's assets have been transmitted."

"I had no idea." Her father's voice was a whisper. "To think I liked Winchester and wanted you to marry him."

"Can we make him pay?"

Darrogh raised an eyebrow. "Justice always finds a way."

"Henry Kingsley left me with a back door into Nethercott's bank." Savis tapped a few keys on the computer. "A couple of strokes and the money is transferred back to Creighton's."

"As easy as that?" Sir Robert tilted his head. "That's amazing."

"I also have access to Nethercott's banking records. Give me permission, and a few hours, and I'll be able to tell you what is happening with his funds. There should be proof of his association with Albirsion Corporation."

"Do it." Sir Robert straightened his shoulders and stood. "I refuse to be held hostage by this group, human or not. I want them stopped."

Tamsin smiled. It was good to see her father take a stand against these people. Threats against her and the bank had taken their toll. Now, he was ready to fight back and combat the Albirsion Corporation. They were no more than thugs that had to be defeated.

"Tamsin, I want you by my side when I confront Kingsley." Her father looked at Darrogh. "You had better come too. I don't think we'll have any trouble from Henry, but I never expected him to steal from me either. I'm not taking any chances."

Tamsin followed Sir Robert out of her office and waited while Darrogh spoke to Savis before joining them. She raised an eyebrow at him once they were in her father's office. She knew that she wanted Winchester to pay for his actions, but she didn't want Darrogh to kill him.

"I hope you weren't arranging something violent for Winchester." Her voice was low enough that only Darrogh could hear.

"Do you wish it?"

"No."

Sir Robert broke into their conversation. "What's the plan?"

Darrogh straightened away from Tamsin. "I asked Savis to do a thorough search of Nethercott's records too."

"The only thing Savis will find is that I was a fool to put my trust in Henry Kingsley."

Darrogh cleared his throat. "It has been my experience that if a person has done one wrong, they are more than likely to have committed several."

"I suppose you've had a lot of contact with criminals." Her father's tone was reflective. "Does that mean you expect to find other irregularities in our records?"

"More than likely." A muscle tightened in Darrogh's jaw. "The people of your planet do not always behave with honor."

Her father sighed and sank into the chair behind his desk. "What other surprises do you think there are?"

"Savis is correcting all that has happened at Creighton's. I am certain he will find that Nethercott has not been totally honest in his own bookkeeping. If possible, Savis is going to see if there is a way to bring Nethercott's illegal activities to the attention of the authorities without implicating Creighton's."

"That's a wonderful plan." Tamsin felt a rush of relief. At least he didn't intend to hurt the man.

"Nethercott has been skirting the law for a while." Her father's voice was resigned. "There have been rumors for years, but no one was able to prove it. After Winchester's father stepped down as chairman, talk died down. I just assumed Winchester had straightened everything out."

"Instead, he made it worse," Tamsin said.

"Now that we know what has happened, we'll be on guard in the future." Her father picked up his phone and pushed a couple of numbers. "Kingsley, in my office now."

"After I fire him, I need you to escort him from the building. Make certain he doesn't have a chance to call anyone, or tamper with the computers."

At that moment there was a knock on the door.

"Come," her father ordered.

Henry Kingsley entered, hesitating a second, when he noticed her and Darrogh. Tamsin almost felt sorry for the man. She'd been on the receiving end of her father's wrath more than once, and she'd never done anything as serious as Kingsley had. Sir Robert Creighton wasn't a man who tolerated being thwarted in his personal or business life.

Her father waited until Henry had shut the door before speaking. "Some serious allegations have been made against you, Henry."

Henry straightened his necktie. "I'm certain they're false."

"How long have you been stealing from me?" Her father raised a hand when Henry opened his mouth. "Don't bother to deny it. I've seen the proof. What I want to know is why I shouldn't have you arrested right now?"

Chapter 20

"You've been siphoning money away from Creighton's. Why?" Sir Robert made the accusation in a stern voice.

Darrogh watched Henry Kingsley for a reaction. The man's eyes widened and then he looked toward the door. Darrogh moved fast. He blocked the exit before Kingsley had a chance to turn around. He leaned against the door and glared at the traitor. The only reason he was still standing was because Tamsin had asked for no violence.

"Sir Robert asked you a question." Darrogh's voice was harsh.

Kingsley wiped his hand over his brow. "You're mistaken. I would never steal from you."

"We have the evidence of your theft. How could you?" Tamsin's voice was filled sadness. "My father treated you like family."

Henry's lip curled. "I was no more than an errand boy. The minute you wanted something, I had to stop everything and get it for you immediately."

"She's my daughter." Sir Robert's voice was filled with exasperation. "If you were in need, I would have done the same."

Henry shook his head. "I asked you for money and you refused to help."

"You wanted one hundred thousand pounds and no questions asked. You can't expect someone to hand over that kind of money without a reason." Sir Robert ran his hand through his grey hair. "I offered you ten thousand. You refused."

"After all of the years of service, you should have considered it a bonus." Henry's voice rose.

"So it's my fault?" Sir Robert scoffed. "You need to take responsibility for your actions."

"I did what was necessary."

"You stole money." Sir Robert leaned back in his chair. "What was it? Gambling?"

"You gave me no choice." Henry lifted his chin. "I would have paid it back."

"What about the funds you transferred to Nethercott's Bank? Was that personal too?"

"The bank was going to be taken over by the Albirsion Corporation anyway. All I did was quicken the process."

"I never expected this kind of betrayal from you." A shudder went through Sir Robert. "You're fired. Consider the fact that I'm not reporting you to the police, as your severance pay."

"You won't get away with this." Henry Kingsley's face contorted with anger. "The people I work with are very powerful. Tamsin isn't safe, and the bodyguards you've hired won't be able to stop their attack."

"You are a fool if you think Albireons can defeat Hunters." Darrogh spoke through clenched teeth. "You had Tamsin followed for the past several months. Was that out of concern for her safety?"

"The Corporation needed to know her whereabouts."

Darrogh clenched his hands into fists. Honor and the Sacred Code demanded that Kingsley die. Kingsley's every action since joining forces with the Albireons had put Tamsin's life in danger. Tamsin shook her head at him. He exhaled and forced himself to relax.

Patience was necessary.

He would deal with Kingsley later.

"That makes it worse for you." Darrogh's tone was a threat. "The people you work with will not tolerate failure. They are not to be trusted. You would be best to give us everything you know and ask for our protection."

"From you?" Kingsley snorted. "You lost Tamsin in Beauvie's, and it was sheer luck that you found her. Remember, I have the pictures to prove it."

"You also sold those photos to the papers." Tamsin's voice shook with outrage. "What did I ever do to you?"

"You were out clubbing every night. It was only a matter of time before you became front-page news."

"Enough." Sir Robert's command reverberated through the office. "Pack your things and leave. Darrogh will escort you out. You've done enough damage already."

Darrogh followed Kingsley to his office and watched as he took a couple of pictures from his desk before grabbing his coat. Once Henry Kingsley had left the building, Darrogh returned to Sir Robert's office. Tamsin was seated beside her father and Savis was leaning over both of them pointing at the computer screen.

Tamsin looked up.

She smiled and reached a hand out to him.

A wave of pleasure shot through him. A Hunter was usually only welcomed when there was a need for him to protect or fight. He had always accepted his role as a warrior and had never desired anything else. It was a new sensation to have someone happy just because he was there.

"What have you found?" Darrogh asked after he shut the office door.

Savis looked up. "The firewall around Nethercott's outgoing transactions will take days to break through."

"We don't have that much time." Exasperation filled Tamsin's voice. "We have to find out what they did with the bank's money."

"Our money has been transferred back." Sir Robert frowned. "Isn't that enough?"

"No." Tamsin pushed away from the desk. "We need to follow the trail. That's the only way we'll find the people who are responsible for this corruption."

"The Albireons will have covered their tracks." Savis sat on the edge of the desk. "This is not the first planet they've taken over."

"What can we do?" Tamsin asked.

Darrogh sensed the frustration that flowed through her. His only goal was Tamsin's safety. The flow of money through this planet's institutions did not concern him. The Albireons must not find her. She would never live through their brutal experimentation. He knew without a doubt, that if Tamsin died, so would he.

"This is a sophisticated firewall that I have never seen on Earth before."

"It's alien?" Tamsin frowned. "How can you tell?"

"It uses codes and fail-safes that have not been developed on Earth yet."

Tamsin's eyes narrowed. "This is proof that the Albireons are in control of Nethercott Bank."

"Perhaps." Darrogh kept his voice neutral. If the Albireons were unafraid to use advanced computer technology, then they considered themselves to be protected. "What are the safeguards?"

"If we try to infiltrate without a password, then the whole system shuts down. It collapses into itself and would be beyond repair." Savis gave Darrogh an intense look. "We cannot breach the firewall until we are certain we can get in."

"There has to be a way." Tamsin sighed.

"The firewall is deployed at Nethercott's, so that means someone there has access." Savis straightened away from the desk. "If we find out who controls it and get their entry code, then we can infiltrate without their knowledge."

"We could be a ghost in their system." Tamsin tilted her head. "You just need the password?"

Savis nodded. "I'll be able to access everything from here."

"No." Darrogh knew what Tamsin was thinking before she said it. "I will not let you risk your life."

"I want to." Tamsin turned to her father. "There is only one person who would be responsible for this and that is Winchester."

Her father looked undecided. "It could be any one of his employees."

"Winchester would never let someone else near these records." Tamsin tapped a finger on the desk. "He doesn't have an assistant and whenever I visited, he made certain that his computer was shut down. I'm certain that he's the only one who has access."

"You won't be able to get the information if he's that protective." Her father's voice was doubtful.

"He keeps everything on his cellphone or in a small black book locked in his top desk drawer." Tamsin's voice rose in excitement. "His cellphone is always with him, but I have a chance of getting the book."

"It is too dangerous." Darrogh fought back the urge to pull her out of the room and away from here. The longer she stayed in London, the more treacherous things became. She already had Henry Kingsley threatening retribution from the Albireons. If Nethercott guessed her real purpose, there would be no saving her.

"I can handle Winchester."

Darrogh shook his head. "He is not the man you think."

"Really?" Tamsin's eyebrows rose. "I think he's a deceiving low-life with absolutely no moral compass. He's ambitious and will do anything to get what he wants."

"I'm glad you don't harbor any resentment." Her father's voice was dry. "If you had gone through with the wedding, none of this would have happened."

Savis cleared his throat. "The transfer of funds began two years ago."

Sir Robert's shoulders sagged. "He's been stealing from me all that time?"

Savis nodded. "Initially it was done so that a cursory glance at the records would not alert your auditors. In the last year, he has become more aggressive. He would have had everything within a month, and then I suspect you would have been facing criminal charges for misappropriation of funds."

Sir Robert groaned. "What a fool I was to trust him."

"Now do you understand my hostility toward Winchester? Finding him sleeping with Liz was a small betrayal compared to this." Tamsin squeezed her father's arm. "Marrying me would have made his fraud easier. We were a minor roadblock to his ambition."

Her father straightened his shoulders. "That doesn't mean you should endanger yourself. The funds have been transferred back to Creighton's."

"I need to do this." Tamsin leaned close to her father. "If we can trace his connection back to the Albireons, then we can stop the flow of money."

"That has nothing to do with us."

"Everyone in the world will be affected if the Albireons take over Earth." Tamsin looked up at Darrogh. "Remind my father what these monsters are capable of."

Darrogh hesitated. He understood the necessity of stopping the infiltration of the Albireons and defeating them. He did not want Tamsin to get involved. It was enough that he had already experienced the torture and clinical experimentation of these fiends.

"Your father has been told." Savis spoke up. "He has chosen not to believe. Hunters protect women. We do not let them put themselves in danger. We will get the codes another way."

"You also obey women." Tamsin's voice was firm. "I insist on doing this."

The silence in the room was broken by Sir Robert's quiet chuckle.

"It's been a long time since I've seen you this interested in something." Her father leaned over and kissed her cheek. "You can't go alone. You must have someone else with you and an escape plan."

"You are willing to let Tamsin take this risk?" Darrogh's voice held disbelief.

Sir Robert stood. "My daughter has always been stubborn. She'll find a way to do it with or without protection. It's easier to keep her safe, if you go with her."

Darrogh felt the determination that was coursing through Tamsin. Her father was right. Already, she had almost been killed because she had chosen to go out on her own. He might not be lucky enough to rescue her a second time, and after what they had learned about Winchester, he did not want to chance it.

"You will follow my direction." His voice brooked no argument.

"He'll be suspicious if we're together." Tamsin's voice became pleading. "I have to meet him in his office. You can stay outside the bank."

Darrogh shook his head. "It will not give me enough time to reach you if he discovers your true purpose."

"He's a liar and a cheat, but he's never been violent before." Tamsin pushed away from the desk. "I can handle him."

"You have never been caught stealing from him." Darrogh crossed his arms. "If he finds you riffling through his desk, he will know that you are out to hurt him. He has been involved with the Albireons for at least two years. He will have taken precautions."

Tamsin shrugged. "I'll tell him I want a reconciliation."

"Nethercott isn't a fool." Her father shook his head. "You'll have to come up with a better story than that."

Tamsin heaved a sigh. "By the time I get to his office, I'll have everything planned out."

"We need to get the passcode before they discover that we've siphoned the money back to Creighton's, otherwise they will close the system themselves." Savis shut his laptop. "I'm going to stay here and try a couple of other tricks to unlock this firewall."

Darrogh opened the office door for Tamsin. "We will go and meet with Winchester."

She walked into the hallway and grinned back at him. "It'll be fun."

"Be careful." Sir Robert's voice sounded weary. "Getting Winchester is important, but not at the expense of your lives."

"I will protect her."

Darrogh left the office. Tamsin was waiting for him at the top of the stairs. She was tapping her finger on the oak railing, and Darrogh had the sudden urge to grab her close and refuse to let her leave. None of the warnings about Winchester had affected her eagerness to get the password. He understood that she felt betrayed and angered by his actions, but that was no excuse for putting herself in harm's way.

Tamsin was determined to see justice done.

No matter what the cost.

"I will not let you go into Winchester's office without me."

"You made that quite clear." Tamsin started down the stairs. "I can take care of myself."

"I would die if something happened to you." Darrogh spoke in a quiet voice. "We are connected and what happens to one of us, happens to both."

Tamsin stopped her descent. "I hadn't considered that."

"I cannot allow you to walk into this danger alone."

Tamsin turned to him and put her hand on his chest. "A compromise then. I will go into his office and you can wait outside the door. Will that give you enough time to reach me?"

Darrogh nodded. "If you sense danger, then so will I."

Tamsin stood up on her tiptoes and gave him a quick kiss on the cheek. "It's settled. Let's go get the information."

Darrogh fought the urge to touch the cheek she had kissed. It felt as if he had been caressed by lightning-infused pleasure. He shook off the sensation and forced his mind back to the protection of Tamsin. He stilled his breathing, and followed her as she moved through the customers. She headed to the side door and had opened it before he could stop her.

He blocked her way with his arm. "This exit is not being monitored."

"It's quicker." Tamsin dodged under him and out the door. "The sooner I speak with Winchester, the better."

"Let me go first."

Darrogh stepped out the door into a side alley.

It ran the full length of the bank.

One end was the rear of another building that had a junction that led into two other side streets. The other end was the main street. Opposite the bank was a brick building with a number of empty doorways. Darrogh looked up at the camera monitoring the entrance. It was directed toward the rear alley and away from the door.

A tingling sensation raced up his spine.

He held his arm out to stop Tamsin from moving.

Out of the corner of his eye, he caught movement from one of the doors across from them. It was out of range of the camera. He pushed Tamsin back against the building just as the crack of a gun being fired split the air.

Chapter 21

Tamsin's heart froze.

They were being shot at.

A bullet whizzed by Darrogh's head and slammed into the wall beside him. Shards of brick flew off and hit his face. Tamsin gasped when she saw the blood oozing down his cheek. He didn't wince. He continued to stay in front of her and move both of them back toward the building.

"We need help." Darrogh looked up at the rooftop. "I'll hold them off until the others get here."

If only she hadn't been so flippant about her protection. She always took the side door when she left the bank. It was second nature, so she hadn't thought about letting Darrogh set up the surveillance before she took the detour. It was too late for regrets now.

"Who would be so bold to attack in daylight?"

"Albireons." Darrogh spit the word out. "Inside."

"The door has locked behind us."

"Run."

"I can't leave you here alone." Tamsin saw a movement out of the corner of her eye and screamed. "Look out."

Darrogh spun around and blocked the fist that was intended for his jaw. He wrenched the arm high in the air. Tamsin heard the distinct cracking of bone. He twisted the man's neck and then threw the body off to the side.

Another attacker jumped on his back.

Tamsin shuddered with horror.

Every blow to Darrogh's body felt like a physical attack on her. This time, Darrogh spun his body around and slammed into the wall behind him. His attacker was crushed, and his hold on Darrogh loosened as he slid down the wall.

An Albireon reached for her.

She hefted her purse in the air and beat it against the man's outreached arm. Darrogh pulled him away and slammed the man's head against the wall, just as another gunshot rang out. This time the shot whizzed by her head.

She was grabbed by the arm and dragged down the alley toward the main road. She dug the heels of her leather loafers into the cobblestones and pulled her weight back. It had no effect. The man continued to pull her away from Darrogh. A black SUV drove up and stopped so that it blocked the exit.

Tamsin's heart pounded in her chest.

She was being kidnapped.

From behind, she could hear the sound of another body landing on the ground. She pulled at the fingers clasped around her arm just as Darrogh launched himself at the man holding her. He seized the hand that was locked onto Tamsin, and wrenched it from her. She fell backwards just as he freed her. Darrogh grabbed her abductor around the neck and twisted his head. She heard the sickening crunch of his neck being broken.

Darrogh dropped the body.

Two more Albireons jumped out of the car.

Darrogh pulled Tamsin up from the ground. "We need to leave," he said in a calm voice.

Tamsin couldn't avoid looking at the body at her feet. It was Albireon, not human, but that didn't lessen her horror. Her stomach rolled with nausea. Five men had been killed in less than a minute. She tried to move, but her legs were frozen. Darrogh picked her up in his arms and carried her back to the side door. He put her down on her feet in front of the keypad lock beside the door.

"Do you know the combination?"

Tamsin punched in the numbers.

Nothing happened.

She could hear running feet approaching. Darrogh turned and positioned his body in front of her. She sensed him tensing and knew that he was preparing to fight the new attackers. Frantically, she pushed in the code again. Still, the door refused to open. The code must have been changed since she left the bank. She glanced behind her shoulder just in time to see a man running at them with a gun raised. Darrogh took a step forward. Tamsin braced herself for another attack.

Two shots rang out.

Both assailants fell to the ground.

Darrogh looked up to the roof of the bank. She followed his glance and saw the glint of glass. Somehow, Breanon had repositioned himself from his watch at the front door. The SUV at the end of the alley, sped off.

Darrogh turned back to Tamsin and put his hand over hers. "Are you injured?"

She shook her head. "There were so many of them."

"They are dead."

Tamsin looked into his calm eyes and exhaled. It seemed impossible that they had lived through that attack. She wiped away the blood from his cheek. "You're hurt."

"The bullet missed."

"You could have been killed." Her voice shook as she fought back tears.

Darrogh pulled her into his arms and ran a hand down her back. He held her close until her breathing and heartbeat returned to normal. When her panic and shock had subsided, he leaned back and looked down at her.

"I promised to protect you with my life."

"I never expected you to be tested. We should call the police and let them know about the attack."

The side door swung open and Savis rushed out.

Darrogh helped her inside. The whole time he used his body to block her view of the alley. Another shudder went through her as she remembered the men lying dead on the cobblestones. She had always thought herself safe from violence. Now in the space of a three days, she'd experienced more brutality than most people do in a lifetime. She rested her head on Darrogh's chest and let the warmth of his embrace comfort her.

Darrogh spoke in a low voice to Savis. "Make certain they cannot hurt us."

Savis was gone for several minutes. When he returned, his words sent a shiver through her. "Six Albireons and one human at the end of the alley. You need to leave the area."

Tamsin straightened up in Darrogh's arms. "I want to find Winchester. He's responsible for all of this."

"Those were Albireons." Darrogh's voice was low. "Henry Kingsley must have notified them when he left the bank."

Tamsin stepped back from Darrogh. "All the more reason for us to see Winchester. He knows what is happening."

"It is safer if we leave London."

"Not until I have the password to his firewall." Tamsin straightened the collar of her blouse and pulled her jacket down. "Once I have that, I will do whatever you want."

Darrogh looked at Savis. "How important is the code?"

"It will save us at least two weeks."

"They will have covered their tracks by then." Darrogh sighed. "Make certain that Breanon is covering us. Firbin and Jehon can take care of the bodies."

"Do you want me to go with you?"

Darrogh shook his head. "Stay here. Once we have the code, I will pass it to you. Get into their records and do what you need as fast as possible. We do not want them to suspect anything before we have a chance to follow their money trail."

"Understood."

Darrogh took her arm and walked her to the foyer.

She knew that he was upset by her decision, but she couldn't let these people win. It went against everything she believed in. She needed to see this through and get the information that Savis needed. Only then, would they be able to find out how much this organization had penetrated the world's banks. If they were lucky, it was only Nethercott's that they had under their control. She shuddered to think what would happen to the country and the world if more banks were affected. If this organization was determined to destroy Earth, then decimating the planet's economy would be go a long ways toward doing it.

"Did you use the side door to meet Winchester?"

Tamsin shook her head. "I seldom went to see him during the day. I used the side exit because I loved the small restaurant one street over."

Darrogh nodded. "We will not go the normal route to Nethercott's office. We'll take the transit and then backtrack."

Tamsin didn't argue. They walked to the underground and took a circuitous route around the city until they arrived at Nethercott's office. Darrogh wouldn't let her approach the bank until he was certain that no one was following them.

The bank was a stark contrast to Creighton's. Where Creighton's was old brick, wooden trim and Victorian in design, Nethercott's was glass and steel. There were no smiling greetings, just cold, professional courtesy. She was recognized, and when she asked to see Winchester, she was directed to go up in the elevator to the top floor.

Winchester's office was empty.

"It's best if I go in alone." Tamsin kept her voice low. "Knock on the door when he's coming."

"I do not approve." Darrogh scowled. "He could still hurt you."

"I'll yell." Tamsin brushed her hand across his chest. "If he has plans to hurt me, he'll have someone else do it."

"It is dangerous being in the enemy's territory."

Tamsin's eyes widened. She hadn't thought about it like that, but she guessed that Winchester was now truly an enemy. "I will be very careful."

She entered the office and shut the door behind her.

Two full walls of windows surrounded a glass and metal desk. A couple of modern plastic chairs were in front of the desk and two sofas sat against the far wall. A chill raced through her as she took in the starkness of Winchester's work space. It was a true reflection of her ex-fiancé; he was cold and impersonal.

She straightened her shoulders and pushed away from the door. She glanced up to see if there were any security cameras monitoring the office. There were none. She doubted that Winchester allowed anyone to question his actions.

The desk drawer was the best place to look.

She pulled on the handle of the top drawer in the center of the desk. It was locked. She then tried all of the other drawers. They opened, and a quick look through the contents showed no small black book. She felt under each drawer looking for a key to use on the lock. Again, she came up empty.

She bit her lip and looked around the room. Where would he hide a spare key? Winchester didn't trust people, and he was fanatical about having a backup for everything. He would have put a second key somewhere close. There were very few books or decorations in the room and she doubted that he would put a key in anything so obvious.

She looked at the closed door to his private restroom.

Winchester was vain and obsessive about his appearance.

He was constantly checking that his hair was in place and that there was nothing stuck in his teeth. She used to think he spent more time in front of the mirror than doing work. Now that she knew he funded his bank's growth by stealing from Creighton's, she understood why he didn't need to make an effort.

She opened the restroom door. It had a sink, toilet, and two mirrors. One above the sink and one behind the toilet. She ran her fingers along the edges of the mirrors and came away empty. The only other place was the small sink cabinet. She pulled the drawers out and again nothing.

With a frown she gave the room one last look, letting her eyes linger on the expensive hairspray and aftershave that were sitting on the shelf above the sink. There was also a can of cheap deodorant. Winchester only used designer fragrances and sprays. This was out of place.

She shook the can.

It rattled.

She felt along the edges of the can and discovered a false bottom. When she unscrewed it a key fell out. She ran back to the locked desk drawer and inserted the key. It turned in the lock and a click later, the drawer was open.

The black book was on top.

She rifled through the pages until she found a section called Creighton's. She grabbed a pen and paper from her purse and wrote everything down. Then she turned to the Nethercott section and wrote down all of the different passcodes there. Her fingers shook by the time she was done.

She wasn't in the clear yet. She needed to get the key back in its hiding spot before Winchester arrived. She had just finished replacing the can, when she heard Darrogh's knock, followed by his voice in her head.

"Winchester has arrived."

Chapter 22

Tamsin shut the restroom door, scrambled back into the office, and plopped herself down on one of the chairs in front of his desk. She straightened her blouse and jacket, and took a deep breath to slow her breathing.

Winchester entered the room with a scowl on his face. "Do you always bring that goon with you?"

Tamsin fought the urge to jump to Darrogh's defense. Instead, she put her brightest smile on and fluttered her eyelashes. "He makes me feel safe."

"I'd think big and muscular would get old after a while." Winchester pulled out the seat behind his desk. "Why are you here?"

"I've been thinking about our chat yesterday. Did you really mean your suggestion that we try to be a couple again?"

Winchester stopped fiddling with his pen and gave her a penetrating look. "Come to your senses have you?"

"I was attacked."

"When?" Winchester leaned his elbows on his desk.

"That's not important." Tamsin swallowed back her memories of the confrontation in the alley. A part of her wondered if Winchester was aware of the incident. Looking at him across his desk, she found it hard to believe that he would be able to sit here and talk to her calmly if he'd been behind the attack.

Winchester shrugged. "I warned you."

"That's why I'm here." Tamsin clasped her hands together. "If we married, would they leave my father and me alone?"

Winchester leaned back in his chair. "I already told Albirsion Corporation that your answer was no."

"So there's no reasoning with this corporation?" Tamsin's voice was low. "Surely if you went to them, they'd make an exception. The last time we talked, you made it sound as if you had an inside track with them."

"They make the rules." Winchester picked up his pen. "I'm not a fool. I keep my mouth shut and do what they tell me."

"So you're refusing to help."

Winchester tapped the pen on the glass surface of his desk. "My offer to wed you was very generous, especially considering that you're frigid."

Tamsin jumped back as if she'd be slapped. "I didn't want to consummate our relationship until we were married. That doesn't mean I'm frigid."

Winchester smirked. "You couldn't stand to let me touch you."

Tamsin didn't bother to argue. She'd hated his hands on her, and she'd foolishly thought that once they were married that would change. There was no doubting that it was a blessing that she'd found Liz and Winchester together in bed. It had given her a reason to stop the wedding.

"You're right." Tamsin stood. "It was foolish of me to come here."

Winchester's eyes widened. "I'm certain we could work something out."

"Like an open marriage that would let us both go our separate ways." Tamsin shook her head. "Not even for my father's sake am I willing to do that. I'll fight these people on my own."

"They're too powerful."

"Perhaps." Tamsin raised her chin. "At least I'll sleep better knowing I tried to do something."

"You've always been difficult, Tamsin. I can't say it's been a pleasure knowing you."

"We're agreed on one thing." Tamsin turned and left the room.

Darrogh was waiting for her.

She tilted her head.

He gave her a searching look before leading her toward the elevator. They rode down in silence. A sense of peace and safety enveloped her. It felt as if Darrogh was holding her close. Everything she wanted from life was standing right beside her. It had been less than two weeks since she'd first met Darrogh, and yet she felt as if a lifetime of emotions and love had happened in that time.

There was only one man for her.

Darrogh.

They headed for the tube once they were outside. No words were spoken until they were safely inside the train. Darrogh found a seat for her, and then stood in front of her so that his body protected and blocked her from the view of others.

"Did you get it?" She felt the words, rather than heard them.

She handed him the paper she'd written everything on. "We should take this to Savis right away."

Darrogh shook his head. "Too dangerous."

He frowned down at the paper for a few seconds and then folded it. He glanced behind him before shoving it into his front jacket pocket. When he turned back, she could see the tension in his eyes. Something was wrong.

She shifted in her seat to try and look around him.

He took a step closer. "We are being followed."

Her heart beat quickened and she clenched her hands into fists. They'd been so careful in making certain that no one had followed them to Winchester's office. If the Albireons had guessed their purpose, then speed was even more important than before.

"How did they find us?"

"I sensed them the minute we left Nethercott's bank."

"Were they there before we arrived?"

Darrogh shook his head.

There was only one explanation.

"Winchester alerted them." Tamsin closed her eyes. "I tried not to do anything that was suspicious."

"It is not your fault." Darrogh braced himself as the train came into the next station. "We will exit and take a taxi to your house."

Tamsin was jostled by the crowd on the platform as they left the train. People were everywhere. She felt a hand grab her, and looked up into the hairless face of a man wearing a black overcoat and hat. He looked identical to the men who had attacked them in the alley. Panic rose inside her. Before she could react, Darrogh pulled her close and elbowed the offender in the face.

He half carried her up the stairs and out of the station. Once outside, he hailed a cab and rushed her into it. Only when they were moving, did he release his hold on her.

"Are you hurt?"

Tamsin shook her head. "They're getting bolder."

"They are desperate." Darrogh pulled out the crumpled sheet of paper she had handed him earlier with the passwords on it. "I have already sent Savis the information. He will have found his way into their financial records by now."

"So everything will be okay." Tamsin sagged back against the seat.

"Not until I get you out of London." Darrogh clasped her hand. A frisson of heat went up her arm. She leaned her head against his chest and let his strength ease her fears. "I will always protect you."

"Thank you." Tamsin looked into his eyes. "When I sat across from Winchester today, all I could think about was how lucky I was to have found out about his betrayal before I married him."

"He is a man without honor."

"I should never have agreed to marry him." Tamsin lowered her voice. "I realized today that you're the only man I want to be with. I love you."

A glint of excitement flared in Darrogh's eyes.

His hold on her tightened.

"I am bonded with you." His voice was husky. "It would be an honor to be your mate. I will not ask you to make such a serious decision until we have defeated the Albireons and you are safe."

Before Tamsin could reply, the taxi came to a stop. She looked out the window and saw that they had arrived at her house. With a sigh, she straightened up and waited until Darrogh had paid the cabbie. He stepped outside the cab and assessed the area, before helping her out of the vehicle. Jehon joined them at the sidewalk.

"The Albireons have set up a position in the rear."

Darrogh nodded and held the front door open for her to pass through. "They will not attack as long as it is daylight. We will keep them under surveillance."

Jehon locked the door behind them. "We also have guests."

Tamsin frowned. "I wasn't expecting anyone."

"The police have returned."

A shudder went through her. Had they found evidence that linked her to Saxby's death? With a trembling hand she brushed her hair back from her face and let out a shaky breath. She had no memory of what had happened in the apartment, and Peter Newton had already given a statement that she wasn't there.

The police had to be here for another reason.

It must be the attack in the alley.

"I'm ready." She walked into the reception room.

DI Milton and DS Barton were standing with their backs to the fireplace and notebooks in hand. When she entered the room, DI Milton walked toward her.

"We have more questions."

Tamsin sat on her couch and motioned for DI Milton to sit across from her. The police officer shook her head. She looked down at her notes.

"We are having difficulty recovering CCTV footage from Saturday night. Do you have any idea why that might be?"

For a second Tamsin thought she'd misheard the inspector. "Are you suggesting that I tampered with video feeds?"

"Someone did."

"It wasn't me." Tamsin smiled. "I know finances not computers. I wouldn't have a clue where to start."

"What about your security team." The inspector's expression was grim as she glanced at Darrogh who was standing beside Tamsin. "I suspect that your team would do anything to protect you."

"That is true." Darrogh's voice was cold. "We would die to protect Tamsin."

"That's hardly an answer." DI Morton frowned. "Does your protection include murder or covering up a homicide?"

"I am a warrior. I follow the Sacred Code."

"Is that a yes?"

"We do not murder innocent people. There is no honor in that."

Tamsin cleared her throat. "He answered your question. Is there anything else I can help you with?"

DI Morton looked at her. "Was there something you forgot to tell us about Saturday night?"

"I told you everything that I know." Tamsin shook her head. "George was a friend. Surely you have other suspects besides me?"

DS Barton flipped her notepad closed. "That's the problem. We have too many suspects and no evidence that anyone was ever at his apartment Saturday night."

"You're certain it wasn't suicide?"

DS Barton and the inspector exchanged a look.

Tamsin held her breath as she waited.

"It's possible," DI Morton admitted. "In my gut, I don't believe it. He wasn't the type of man to kill himself."

"How do you know that?" Tamsin's voice was hesitant.

"There was no suicide note, and nothing in his apartment to indicate remorse for his violent treatment of women." DI Morton tapped her notebook. "It's more probable that one of his victims took their revenge."

"He does not deserve your efforts." Darrogh's voice was harsh.

"It's my job to find the truth."

Darrogh crossed his arms. "You will not find it here."

"My instinct tells me different." The inspector paused for a few seconds and then turned toward the door. "Without any evidence, I have nothing to go on."

When the detectives had left the house Tamsin leaned back. "For a few seconds I thought you were going to tell her the truth."

"I would not have lied," Darrogh admitted. "I would have hated to leave you here alone, but I would have escaped. Your laws cannot hold me."

There was a loud pounding on the front door.

Darrogh motioned for Jehon to check it out. He came back with Peter Newton. Newton's face was pale and his hands shook as he put his camera down on the table. Tamsin guided him to a chair and asked Jehon to get some water. When Peter had gulped back the liquid, he put the glass down with a rattle.

"Henry Kingsley has just been killed by a hit and run driver."

Chapter 23

"What happened?" Tamsin asked.

"I followed Kingsley after he left the bank." There was a tremor in Peter's voice. "He made a phone call so I thought he might lead me to his contacts."

"That was a dangerous plan," Darrogh said. "Did they see you?"

Peter shook his head. "I was too far away. They talked for a few minutes and then his contacts left. I was about to follow them, when I heard the screeching of tires behind me. I ducked into a doorway and started clicking pictures."

"You saw it happen. How horrible." Tamsin touched Peter's arm. "Did you get a good look at the person behind the wheel? That should help the police find the driver."

Peter held up his camera and started to scan through the pictures he'd taken. The images flickered by like a movie and Darrogh was not surprised when he saw that the man behind the wheel was wearing a black coat and black hat. His face was emotionless as he raced toward Henry and ran him over.

"The Albireons are covering their tracks."

Darrogh had known it was only a matter of time before the Albireons took notice of their activities and tried to eliminate them. The attack this morning had been their first real attempt to silence Tamsin. The shooting of the tire had only been a warning and scare tactic. There would be no restraints now that they knew Henry Kingsley's sabotage had been discovered.

They had waited too long to leave London.

"It is not safe for us here." Darrogh straightened away from the camera.

At that moment, Firbin entered the room. "Breanon is in position at the rear."

"What about the front? We need a clear line on the house from the park," Darrogh said.

"I will go and take up a position." Firbin left the room just as Kerm entered with Savis.

"Were you successful?" Darrogh asked.

"Yes." Savis put his laptop down on the table in front of Tamsin. "There is a direct connection with Winchester Nethercott. Once the Creighton's funds reached his bank, he transferred them into Albirsion Corporation banks."

"You were able to stop that from happening I hope?" Tamsin's voice cracked.

"Yes, but I found other irregularities in Nethercott's files." Savis glanced up at Darrogh, who nodded for him to continue. "Nethercott has been laundering money from illegal operations setup through Albirsion. He has been instrumental in increasing their wealth. There was more."

Tamsin sat down and shut her eyes for a few seconds. "Tell me the rest."

"Nethercott has been systematically draining other banks around the world of their funds just like he did with Creighton's."

"The Albireons plan to control Earth's global economy." There was no doubt in Darrogh's mind that this was one of the thrusts in their takeover of the planet. "They have probably been planning this for years."

"They do not know that I have infiltrated them." Savis's voice was quiet. "It will take me a few hours, but I should be able to plant a backdoor into their system that they will not find. That way I will have future access and time to correct what they have done."

Darrogh did not hesitate. "Do it. We need to stop them wherever possible."

Savis reached for his computer. "I have left the evidence of Winchester's money laundering on the books. I can correct the money siphoning from other banks just like I did at Creighton's, but the best way to stop it from happening again, is to stop Winchester."

Darrogh did not have a problem with seeing the man pay for his actions. "What do you propose?"

"Leak evidence of the money laundering," Savis said.

Tamsin frowned. "Is that wise?"

Savis picked up his computer. "The alternative is to kill Winchester, but that will leave his contacts alive."

"I don't want him killed." Tamsin was definite. "Involving the police isn't going to stop Albirsion Corporation."

"It will delay the Albireon plans and stop the flow of money to them," Savis's explained.

"So Winchester, and the people he is laundering money for, will be arrested." Darrogh liked the idea. "Send the information anonymously to the authorities. If they are not controlled by the Albireons, then they will stop the illegal activity."

Savis nodded. "I will continue to monitor the Albireons' finances so that we will know when they find new sources of money."

"We will shut down those operations as they occur." Darrogh nodded.

"It is a good plan."

"Is it necessary to send Winchester to jail?" Tamsin's voice was unsure.

"He committed fraud. Do not your laws have a penalty for this?" Darrogh asked.

"I suppose it is fitting." Tamsin sighed. "It's impossible to believe. Nethercott's used to be such an upstanding institution."

"Winchester had a choice. He decided to join with the Albireons."

"You're right." There was still doubt in Tamsin's voice. "He might not know how horrible Albirsion Corporation is."

"The people he launders money for are criminals." Savis's voice was matter of fact.

"He is also the one who alerted the Albireons that you had been in his office." Darrogh clenched his hands at the thought of what might have happened to Tamsin if he had not been with her. "That is the reason your house is under surveillance and we are being followed."

Tamsin looked up at Darrogh. "He couldn't know what they intend to do."

"He knows." Darrogh waited until he saw acceptance of the truth about Winchester's betrayal in Tamsin's eyes.

Tamsin gave him a shaky nod. "You're right. I told him that I was attacked and he showed no surprise."

"He needs to be stopped."

"The Albireons are preparing to attack." Kerm glanced toward the windows. "It will be dark soon."

"You cannot stay here." Darrogh's stomach tensed as a sense of unease shot through him. "Savis, tell Ardal your plans and then execute them. Ask for reinforcements as soon as possible. I need to get Tamsin away from London."

"We still have a house in the north of England." Kerm's voice was curt. "When we were hiring out as mercenaries, it was essential to have a safe location in every country. It hasn't been used in the last year, but it should be protection until we can get more Hunters here."

"We will go there." Darrogh turned to Tamsin. "Pack only a change of clothing. We leave in five minutes."

"Can't we wait until morning?" There was obstinate refusal in Tamsin's voice.

Darrogh sent her a wave of calm and reassurance. There was no time to debate. The Albireons were close to attacking and he needed to get her out of this house.

"No."

Tamsin gave him a long searching look.

He sensed her unease.

A second later, it was gone. She nodded and left the room. Only then, did he turn to the others.

"What is the best way to get out of London unseen?"

"The underground." Peter Newton spoke in a decisive voice. "Let me see the map of the London tube system."

Savis pulled up the chart on his laptop.

Peter looked at the screen. "There are entries into hidden tunnels beneath the city. If you can access one of them, then you will be able to avoid detection."

Peter pointed to Chancery Lane Station. "There is a secret entrance to an underground tunnel that will connect you with this station. It's only about half a mile long, but if we can get you there without being followed, then the Albireons won't know where you are."

"What do we do once we are there?" Darrogh asked.

"Stay on the tube until the Central Line ends at Epping Station. From there, you'll have to take a car and get on the A1. That will take you north."

"We'll need a car waiting for us."

"I will arrange one to be there. I'll pull Tamsin's vehicle up to the front of the house and drive you." Kerm left the house.

Darrogh looked up from the map that he had committed to memory. "They are planning to attack tonight. I can feel it in my bones. You will have to hold them off."

"Not a problem. I will go and get the weapons ready," Jehon said.

"I'm coming with you." Peter Newton stood. "You'll never get access to the hidden underground system without me."

"It will be dangerous." Darrogh appreciated the offer of help, but he did not want the man risking his life. "I might not be able to protect you."

"I can take care of myself." Peter's voice was strong. It was obvious he had recovered from the harrowing experience of seeing Kingsley run down in broad daylight. "I didn't believe you guys at first. I can't deny what I saw with my own eyes today, though."

Tamsin came back into the room. She was carrying a small leather backpack over her shoulder and had changed into jeans, comfortable shoes and a woolen sweater.

"I'm ready." She pulled her hair back into a ponytail. "Are we driving?"

"Peter is coming with us. It is risky, but we need to get to Furnival Street near the Chancery Lane tube station." Darrogh took the pack from Tamsin. "We will drive there. It will take the Albireons a few minutes to follow. Once we reach the underground, we should be able to lose them."

Jehon came back with a couple of pistols that he handed to Darrogh. He also added a box of bullets. Peter's eyes widened when he saw the weapons and he shook his head. "I'm not going to ask if they're legal."

"These are primitive but effective." Darrogh hid one of the guns in his jacket. The bullets and second pistol he put in Tamsin's pack. "We use what we must. If they attack, then I will defend."

Tamsin shuddered. "Let's hope we can outwit them."

"You need to delay the Albireons from following us." Darrogh looked at Jehon. "Use whatever tactics you think necessary, including shooting out the tires on their vehicles."

"I will alter the angle of the CCTV cameras at Furnival and Epping Station," Savis added. "If they have access to the video feed that should stop them from finding your route."

"The main goal is to delay until Ardal's reinforcements arrive." Darrogh turned to Peter. "Ready?"

Peter picked up his camera. "When I've got you two away safely, I'm going to lay low for a few days. It sounds as if you're planning a battle."

They left the house by the front door.

Darrogh could feel the eyes on them as they climbed into Tamsin's car. Kerm sped off the moment the door shut, and swerved around cars on his way to Furnival. When they reached Chancery Lane, Kerm barely stopped as he let them off at the corner of Cursitor Street. Construction was on both sides of the road and only pedestrian traffic was able to get through. This would make it impossible for anyone to pursue them in a car.

Kerm sped off. Darrogh took Tamsin's elbow and led her down the walkthrough that went into Cursitor. Peter followed. When they reached Furnival Street, Peter took the lead, stopping at a building with a black loading door. Tamsin leaned against the building and took a deep breath.

Peter rummaged in his pockets and pulled out a ring heavy with keys.

Darrogh stood guard in front of both of them and looked over his shoulder. No one had followed them. They were safe for the moment, but they could not delay.

"We cannot stay outside long."

"Give me a second." Peter started flipping through his keys. He stopped at a small bronze-colored one and inserted it into the door's lock. The door opened and he went in. Darrogh motioned for Tamsin to follow. He gave another cursory look up and down the road and when he was certain no one had seen them, he entered and shut the door behind him.

Peter turned the lock in the door. "We don't need anyone getting curious."

"This is the old telephone tunnels." Tamsin's voice was a hushed whisper. "How did you get access here?"

"I did some security work for the group that owns it. They were having problems with trespassers." Peter moved his hand in front of a motion sensor and the lights came on. "When the work was finished, I kept a key. You never know when something like that might come in handy."

"How far do we have to go?" Tamsin shivered.

There was a spiral staircase a few feet in front of them and Peter started down it. "It's less than a mile."

Tamsin followed and Darrogh brought up the rear.

Their footsteps on the metal stairs were the only sound. No one was following them. When they reached the bottom, the first thing that Darrogh noticed was the damp, musty smell. His nose also detected a faint odor of diesel. The roar of trains could be heard above them.

"How long has this place been abandoned?" Darrogh glanced up at the ceiling. Bright lights glowed at regular intervals.

"Years." Peter started to walk along a curved tunnel.

"You mentioned trespassers." Tamsin stumbled against a coil of wire. "Do they still monitor it?"

Peter shrugged. "They keep it locked and over time, people forget that these tunnels ever existed."

Tamsin reached out and took Darrogh's hand. He sensed her unease and sent her reassurance. The sooner he had her above ground, the better. Huge cables ran down both sides with a wide area for walking down the middle.

"We need to move fast." Darrogh turned to Tamsin. "Can you keep up?"

She nodded and took off at a jog ahead of them. Peter followed and Darrogh brought up the rear. They covered the distance in about ten minutes, passing metal switching stations, an abandoned cafeteria, and a nursing station along the way. The tunnel forked at a juncture with a set of stairs and a lift on one side.

"This is where we go up." Peter leaned against the wall wheezing. "The lift takes us up to the train platform at Chancery Lane station."

Peter used his key to unlock the metal cage that covered the lift. Once inside, the same key started the elevator's ascent. When it came to a stop, Peter raised his hand before opening the door.

"We exit onto the end of the platform. If we move quickly, no one will notice. Ready?"

Tamsin nodded.

Darrogh readied himself for a possible attack.

The door opened and they exited just as a train whizzed by them. They'd been lucky. The platform was clear, and no one had seen them. Peter locked the lift and then moved with them to the edge of the platform to wait for the next train. When it arrived, Peter stepped back.

"Aren't you coming?" Tamsin asked.

Peter shook his head. "It's best I go into hiding for a while. When the dust settles I'll be back for that job at Creighton's."

"You deserve it." Tamsin smiled up at the man. "Be careful."

Peter nodded. "Good luck. I'll be waiting to hear what happened once everything has cleared up."

Darrogh nodded and then got into the train with Tamsin. There was an empty seat and they both sat. He kept an eye on the platform until the train left and then he scanned the passengers in the car. No one had followed them. He eased back against the seat and pulled Tamsin close. She put her head on his chest and closed her eyes.

A surge of protectiveness raced through him. She trusted him to keep her safe and he was not going to fail. It had been close back at her house. He could not allow that to happen again. Tamsin's life was more important than defeating the Albireons. When he was certain that they were not followed onto the train, Darrogh contacted Kerm through mind connect.

"Did you get the vehicle?"

"It is parked across from Epping Station. It is blue with a white stripe along its side."

"Did the Albireons follow?"

"No." Kerm hesitated a second before continuing. *"Firbin and Breanon killed a number of them before they had a chance to pursue you."*

A nerve tightened in Darrogh's jaw. *"Were there any repercussions?"*

"They used silencers and the bodies have been dealt with."

"I will contact you once we arrive at the safe house."

Forty-five minutes later they pulled into Epping Station. Tamsin let Darrogh lead her out of the building, and she waited while he looked for the vehicle that Kerm had described. He saw it immediately and they walked over to it. The key was hidden under the wheel well and once it was unlocked, he and Tamsin climbed into the small car.

There was a map on the seat and the GPS had been set up. Within seconds, he was driving north. There was silence in the vehicle until they had reached the M1. That's when Tamsin reached over and touched his arm.

"It seems like forever that I've been waiting for us to be alone." The huskiness of her voice sent a shiver of awareness through Darrogh. Every nerve in his body tingled at her nearness. "Now we can talk."

"What about?"

"What happens to us after we're safe?" Tamsin stretched her legs out in front of her.

"That is your decision."

Darkness surrounded them inside the car. The only illumination was the blue glow of the dashboard light and yet Darrogh could see every nuance of Tamsin's surprise as she sat up straight in her seat. She turned to him.

"You weren't kidding when you said that women rule on the planet you're from."

"Hunters do not lie." Darrogh looked over his shoulder before passing the vehicle in front of him. After that, the road stretched empty before them.

"I'm just realizing that now." Tamsin clasped her hands together. "What if I want you to stay with me forever?"

"I will always be with you." Darrogh cleared his throat. "It would be an honor if you chose me for your mate."

"Is that the same as marriage?"

"There is no formal ceremony." Darrogh had difficulty breathing. "There is only one mate for a Hunter. I know it is your custom to marry."

"That is how we make the commitment between two people, binding."

Silence followed her words.

Darrogh sensed that Tamsin was expecting something more from him. He wished that he had paid more attention to his fellow Hunters when they had mated. It might have given him some idea of what a woman expected. Instead, he'd been fearful and doubtful. He knew nothing about women or matters of love. What he did know, was that he could not lose Tamsin.

Darrogh's heart started to race. It felt like he was on the edge of a cliff awaiting orders to jump off. Tamsin was his pair bond. He was connected to her on every level and trusted her completely. Whatever her decision, he would abide by it.

"I feel your essence with every cell in my body." Darrogh's looked at Tamsin. "It would be an honor to spend my life with you as your mate. Will you marry me?"

"I thought you'd never ask."

He could see Tamsin's grin in the muted dashboard light.

"Yes, I will be your wife."

Chapter 24

Tamsin was thankful when they pulled up to a small farmhouse after four hours of driving. It was a moonless night, and darkness enveloped them. They were miles from the main motorway and had reached their destination on roads that were narrow and winding. It was isolated and private.

"Will we be safe here?" Tamsin undid her seatbelt.

"We were not followed." Darrogh turned the engine off and looked at her. "It is only a matter of time before the Albireons know the general area we are hiding in, though."

"So the answer is no." Tamsin opened the car door. "How long before they find us?"

"There are other Hunters coming to help us. They should reached us before the Albireons do." Darrogh opened the house door and switched on the lights. "I will drive the car into the barn. We do not need to advertise that we are here."

Tamsin nodded as she looked around the small house. It was sparsely furnished with a couch, two easy chairs, and a dining table with six seats. There was a small kitchen off to the side and three doors exiting from the main room. She opened the closed doors. Two were bedrooms with a double bed in each. The third opened onto a bathroom.

She rubbed her arms at the slight chill in the air. The far wall of the house had a small fireplace that was set with kindling and logs. She longed to light the fire, but she thought it best to wait for Darrogh. There might be a concern about smoke coming from the chimney. She looked around the walls to see if there was some kind of thermostat for heat. She found one near the entry to the kitchen, and she cranked it up. They might be fugitives and in hiding, but that didn't mean they couldn't be comfortable.

She turned back to the main room when she heard the door open. Darrogh was standing there with her pack in one hand. He shut the door and then pulled her close. It was as if he sensed her unease and was trying to comfort her. With a sigh, she snuggled into him, letting his body heat warm her.

"You need to sleep." Darrogh's voice was a low rumble. "I will stand guard."

"You'll be exhausted tomorrow." Tamsin looked up at him. "You said we'd be safe tonight. This may be the last opportunity for us to be alone together for a while."

Darrogh didn't speak for several seconds.

She held her breath.

She wanted to stay in Darrogh's arms all night long. Even in the midst of danger, all she craved was him. She longed to make love with this man whose very presence drove her crazy; to be one with him.

Darrogh nodded. "You can take the main bedroom. I'll take the other one."

Tamsin's mouth dropped open. "You can't be serious."

Darrogh frowned. "Do you want the other bedroom?"

She swatted his arm. "I want you and me in the same bed."

Darrogh's eyes widened. "Tonight?"

"Is there a reason why we can't? We're officially engaged now."

"Do you not want to wait until we are married?" Darrogh cleared his throat. "Is that not the custom in your country?"

"Seventy years ago." Tamsin shook her head. "You can't expect me to wait that long."

"It is as you wish."

"We'll take the first room." Tamsin grabbed his arm. "I intend to spend the rest of the night in your arms."

She pulled open the door and dragged him in behind her. His reluctance was giving her doubts. "Do you not want to be with me?"

Darrogh closed the door. "I desire it more than anything else."

Tamsin kicked off her shoes and pulled her sweater over her head. "Aren't you going to take your clothes off?"

Darrogh nodded and threw his jacket onto a nearby chair. He started to unbutton his shirt with fingers that fumbled and missed. Tamsin undid her jeans and let them slide to the floor. She stood in front of him in bra and panties, and he still hadn't finished undoing his shirt. She pushed his fingers away and unfastened the buttons before pushing it off his shoulders.

He was magnificent.

Every inch of him was muscle and sinew.

She let her fingers brush across his chest, noting the numerous long scars that crisscrossed him. He trembled beneath her touch and a sweet ache twisted deep inside her. This was the man she was meant to be with. She'd known it from the first moment they'd met. She'd fought the attraction, tried to run away and ignore their connection, and still he was there for her. Protecting and defending her, no matter what she did.

Overwhelming love filled her.

Wanton need consumed her.

Her lips roamed over his chest, kissing each scar as she made her way up to his neck. She stood on her toes and reached for his mouth. He pulled her close. As their lips met, a deep moan rose from Darrogh, and Tamsin found herself lost in the sensations that he stirred within her. Time and place were a blur as together they tasted and savored each other.

When the kiss ended, Tamsin rested her forehead against Darrogh's shoulder. "You have too many clothes on."

"Is it your wish that I undress?" His voice was a husky whisper.

"That's usually the way it's done, unless you've some strange custom on your planet for making love?"

"I have never done this before."

Tamsin's breath caught in her throat. "I thought you meant that you only committed to one woman. I just assumed that you had made love before."

Darrogh eased away from her. "Until I came to Earth, I had never even been close to a woman."

Tamsin's eyes widened. "Never?"

Darrogh shook his head before undoing his boots. He kicked them off and then unzipped his pants. They dropped to the floor and he stepped out of them. Tamsin inhaled a sharp breath. If she'd thought he was gorgeous without his shirt, she'd been mistaken. The full glory and beauty of the man was now evident.

"Should you not also undress?" Darrogh slipped the straps of her bra over her arms.

Tamsin unhooked it.

Then, she slipped her panties over her hips and kicked them off.

Darrogh stood as if frozen. His chest rose and fell in rapid motion and his fingers were clenched into fists at his side. She sensed his hesitation, so she reached for his hand and brought it up to her breast and moved it against her sensitive skin. She moaned as a pulse of need went through her.

"You like that." Darrogh brushed his thumb across her nipple.

Her knees went weak.

"It might be safer if we continued in bed." Her voice was low.

Darrogh wrapped his arm around her back and picked her up in his arms. She could feel his heavy arousal against her body, and moist heat bathed her inner core. He gave her a lingering kissed that promised the world, before he laid her on the bed. She reached up and stroked a hand down his engorged member, enjoying the shock of reaction that shook his body.

He was her mate.

Tonight, they would be one.

Darrogh joined her on the bed. His fingers caressed her skin, tantalizing and exciting her with each stroke. His lips followed. Shivers of ecstasy raced across her body as she struggled to breathe. Darrogh's tongue licked across her abdomen and she arched her back so that she was closer. It was crazy. It was devastating.

"I thought you'd never done this before?" She barely recognized her desire-filled voice.

"I'm a quick learner."

He continued his exploration of her body with his fingers, lips, and tongue, moving lower until he reached her inner thighs.

He paused.

Her fingers clenched the sheets tight as her body waited at the precipice.

He didn't disappoint. He licked and stroked until she shattered and convulsed with ecstasy. She floated down from the heights of pleasure to find herself held close within Darrogh's arms. He was looking down at her with adoration.

"More?"

"Much more of that and you'll kill me." Tamsin reached up and stroked his face. "It's my turn."

When Darrogh opened his mouth to speak, she quietened him with a finger. She sat up and pushed him onto his back so that she could have complete access to him. She began with small kisses on his forehead, eyes, and cheeks. She was gentle as she caressed him with her lips, moving across his neck and down his chest.

Her fingers stroked and kneaded his muscles while her tongue tasted the deliciously salty essence that was Darrogh. Lower and lower she went, reveling in the groans of pleasure that escaped from him.

Excitement pulsed through her as he shook with need. Her hand stroked down his thigh and then moved up to the long length of his manhood.

Soon they would be one.

Darrogh jumped when her tongue circled the tip of his penis. She pushed him back onto the bed when he would have moved away. This was her time to enjoy him, and she meant to taste and lick every inch of him. She kissed down his one thigh and up the other, ending at the juncture between his legs.

He was more than ready.

She ached to feel him inside her.

She straddled him so that the tip of his penis was touching the entrance to her inner core. She paused and looked at him. This was the moment that they had been building to all evening. They would now be joined.

"I love you." Her voice was hoarse. "I need you."

She eased down, letting her body encircle him. "I trust you with every cell of my being."

Then she moved.

Bliss shot through her. As much as she wanted to take this first time with him slow, she couldn't control her hunger. She had to feel him deep within her. She set a pace that sent them both swirling toward completion. Her body exploded with wave upon wave of ecstasy. She collapsed on top of Darrogh and it was several minutes before her breathing had returned to normal.

Darrogh was stroking her back. "I want to do that again."

Tamsin had never experienced anything like their lovemaking. They were still connected and she could feel Darrogh's renewed arousal deep within her. She looked up and gave him a lazy grin.

"I should warn you that men exhaust quickly."

"A Hunter never tires."

His arm tightened around her waist and with an agility that took her breath away, he flipped her onto her back. His hips thrust deep, touching at her sensitive inner core. She spiraled into another orgasm.

Darrogh took control of their lovemaking. He was definitely a quick study and she clasped his shoulders as he took her to heights of pleasure that she had never guessed existed.

Dawn came too soon.

Tamsin stretched her arms above her head and moaned at the delicious ache in her muscles.

All night long, Darrogh had made love to her. He was inexhaustible. He was also very inventive. She smiled as she remembered their lovemaking. She had never been so satiated. She ran her hand down the arm that still held her close to him.

"More?" His voice was sleepy.

"Please."

Darrogh pulled her close and brushed her hair from her face. "I think our connection is deepening."

"Making love with someone has that effect." Tamsin kissed the tip of his nose.

"Can you hear my voice?"

Tamsin's eyes widened and she nodded. His words were clear in her head.

"Know that I will always be with you." Darrogh captured her mouth in a kiss that touched her soul. *"You are my mate. My one and only."*

They moved as one, just as their minds spoke of love. They reached for the heights of ecstasy and together they fell over the precipice as their bodies exploded with rapture. The spark of passion and devotion mingled in their touch and kisses as they continued to make love throughout the morning. Only when the rumbles of hunger were too loud to ignore, did Darrogh get up.

"You need food." He pulled on his pants and shirt. "I will bring you something."

He was gone for several minutes before he came back with coffee and a box of cereal. "There is not much in the house. Once the others have joined us, we will get food."

Darrogh stiffened and walked to the window.

"Do you see someone?"

He shook his head. "Get dressed. I sense danger."

Chapter 25

They were being watched.

He felt it in his bones.

His skin crawled with the warning of peril. It would be foolish to ignore it even though he could not see any evidence of the enemy. They were out there, and if he did not act, they would be attacking them in the house. The only thing that mattered was getting Tamsin to safety.

Last night he had glimpsed paradise.

He refused to let anyone destroy that.

Tamsin was his mate in every sense of the word, and he would protect her with his life. This house had been set up by Lorcan and his unit of Hunters when they had done mercenary work. It had been outfitted with weapon supplies and an escape route. He intended to use everything available to keep Tamsin safe until reinforcements reached them.

He went into the kitchen and kicked the area rug away from the sink. There was a metal latch hidden under the base cupboard trim. It was the entrance to an underground room and tunnel. He pulled it free and then lifted the door up.

Tamsin came into the room. She was straightening her sweater and stopped to look at the open floor. "Can we escape through there?"

"Yes." Darrogh lifted the cover wider. "I want you to hide here. If I do not return, take the tunnel. It leads to another property. You should be able to get help there."

"I'm not leaving without you."

"It is too dangerous." Darrogh went to her. "I need to be able to focus on fighting."

"I could help."

"I would only worry about you." Darrogh took her hands in his. "I am well trained and have survived worse attacks than this."

"That doesn't comfort me." Tamsin's voice was dry. "How many are out there?"

"I do not know." Darrogh led her to the sunken chamber. "There will be other Hunters arriving shortly. They will help."

"You shouldn't have to do this alone. It's my fault that you're here to begin with."

"You have given me a reason to fight."

Darrogh's voice was low. For the first time in his life, he understood what it meant to shield someone you cared about. In the past, it had been about fighting to survive and maintaining his honor. Now it was to protect the one person in the world that completed him. He could not lose Tamsin.

Tamsin started down the wooden ladder that led into the hidden room. "I will hide because you insist, but I won't stay here if I sense that you are in trouble."

"Fair enough." Darrogh pointed to the bolt that was on the inside of the door. "Close this and do not come out until I tell you it is safe."

Once Tamsin was below, and he had heard the bolt pushed in, Darrogh went to the far cupboard of the kitchen. He pushed on the lower backing of the last shelf. It gave way with ease. Behind it was a stash of weapons and ammunition. He loaded the pistols and put two in his waistband. He took two more for each hand along with a couple of full magazines.

His instructions when he had contacted Ardal last night, had been to stay at the farmhouse.

He would hold off the enemy until the others arrived.

Darrogh opened the side door and scanned the horizon. Sheep and cows were grazing in the distance, and the soft purple of heather dotted the field edges. Stone fences bordered the roads and laneways. They would provide good cover. He edged along the side of the house and crouched low before running to one of the outbuildings.

That was when he spotted the first intruder.

It was an Albireon, and he was carrying a rifle.

Darrogh took a deep breath and readied his pistol. Albireons were more fragile than humans and easier to kill. Years on the battlefield had taught him that the best defense was to destroy them as they attacked. Individually, they were easy to kill, but if they were in a large enough group, they could overpower even a Hunter.

The Albireon jumped over one of the stone barriers and was moving through the field toward the house. Darrogh took aim and fired. The man went down. Three more Albireons hopped the fence and started running toward the house. They were making no effort to hide their presence.

Darrogh aimed and shot all of them.

He killed the intruders until he ran out of ammunition. Then he moved out into the fields to attack them directly. He overpowered the first Albireon he came upon and broke his neck. He took his weapon and used it to shoot the next aliens that attacked until it too was empty of bullets.

One by one, he crushed them.

As fast as they came at him, he slew them.

He never let them near the house. Only when the field was filled with lifeless Albireons did he stop. The number of dead was staggering for an assault out in the open. Since they had been on Earth, the Albireons had remained shrouded in secrecy. To see so many of them in one place was unusual and worrisome.

They had no fear of being exposed as extra-terrestrials.

It must mean that capturing Tamsin, and controlling her father's bank, had to be very important to the Albirsion Corporation. They knew she was being guarded by Hunters, so that could explain the large number of men they had sent to attack. The only thing that made Creighton's stand out from other banks was their clientele. Somehow, controlling them had to be part of the Albireon plans to conquer Earth.

Darrogh wiped his bloody hands on his pants. He took a deep breath and glanced around. There were no other Albireons in sight. Still, the familiar whisper of danger was with him. There was only one explanation. Tamsin was at risk. The attackers had been a decoy, sent to keep him away from her.

He left the dead in the field and rushed back to the house.

The door was open.

"*Run.*" He sent the command to Tamsin through mind connect just as the first man rushed toward him. This was not an Albireon, but a human of about the same size and weight as himself. When he raised a gun, Darrogh dived toward the man's knees and the two of them went down together. Darrogh grabbed hold of the hand holding the gun and pushed it into the man's chest. The reverberation of the shot echoed through the small house.

Darrogh rolled off the dead man just as another jumped onto his back. He gripped the man's arms and threw him into the corner of the main living area. When the man stood to attack him again, Darrogh picked up the gun from his first attacker, and shot him dead.

"Enough." An unfamiliar voice rang out. "Stop or the girl dies."

Darrogh's heart skipped a beat.

He turned in the direction of the voice.

A large man with dark hair, and a military type jacket, was holding Tamsin by the arm. The bars on his shoulder identified him as a Major. Behind them, was the open trapdoor with the latch blown off. Darrogh steadied his breathing. Years of training had prepared him for this situation. He would not fail Tamsin.

"What do you want?" Darrogh dropped his gun.

"The girl is necessary for our plans."

"She will not help you." Darrogh's voice was a growl.

"Her father will give us what we want." The man's voice was smug. "They always do."

Tamsin twisted her body in an attempt to free herself. "I won't let him hand over the bank to your organization."

The man shook Tamsin.

She kicked him in the leg.

That was Darrogh's cue. He lunged and pushed the attacker's gun up. At the same time, he chopped down on the arm that was holding Tamsin. The Major shrieked in pain and released her. The Major lowered his arm and aimed his gun at Darrogh. Darrogh wrestled it away and fired the weapon into the man's chest before rushing to Tamsin's side.

"You have to leave."

Tamsin clung to him. She was trembling and did not resist when Darrogh led her to the escape tunnel. The trapdoor was ruined, but the passageway was still open. He would hold off the rest of the attackers while she ran to freedom. Before they could reach the opening, a gunshot rang out.

"Stop." The words were followed by another shot.

Darrogh turned.

He kept Tamsin's body covered by his own.

"I have no problem killing you to get the girl." This man was dressed in a military uniform and he was not alone. Two other similarly garbed men stood behind him.

Darrogh took a step backwards so that Tamsin was within reach of the hatch. He needed her to descend the ladder while he held these men at bay. He sensed her fear and terror. He pushed back another step.

"*Climb down.*" Darrogh mind connected with Tamsin. "*I will hold them off until you are safe.*"

"*I'm not leaving you.*" Tamsin's refusal was a whisper in his mind.

"I will not let you take her." Darrogh readied himself to fight. "I will kill you first."

"I'll save you the effort." The man pulled the trigger.

A burning heat ripped through Darrogh's shoulder. From a distance, he heard Tamsin's scream. She tried to move around him. He held firm. He blocked the pain and Tamsin's terror from his mind, as he raised his weapon and shot the man through the forehead.

Another shot rang out at the same time.

He felt the bullet rip through his arm.

This time he fired two shots in rapid succession. His aim was true and the men fell to the floor. The sound of rushing footsteps brought three more men, dressed in similar military gear, into the house. Darrogh kept Tamsin firmly behind him and shot at the first man. The gun clicked, but no bullet was fired.

He was out of ammunition.

He would have to kill them with his bare hands. He took a step toward the man when the sound of a bullet being fired, rang through the air. Three shots were fired in rapid succession, hitting each of the intruders. They all fell to the ground dead.

Tamsin screamed as two men pushed their way into the farmhouse.

Chapter 26

Tamsin braced herself for another attack.

One of the men started toward them and she stood in front of Darrogh. She wasn't going to let anyone else hurt him. It took her a second to realize that they both looked similar, with dark hair and dark eyes, massive muscles, and height. She knew without being introduced that these were Hunters. They frowned at her and then glanced at Darrogh.

Darrogh dropped his pistol. "It took you long enough to get here."

He'd been shot defending her and he hadn't even flinched. She should have been able to feel his pain, but he had blocked that from her. Her heart beat frantically as she turned to look at his wounds. It was worse than she'd imagined. Tamsin gasped when she saw the blood on her hands.

"He needs a doctor." Tamsin's voice trembled. She had just found Darrogh and she wasn't prepared to lose him now.

"It is a scratch." Darrogh's words sounded slurred.

One of the new arrivals stepped forward. "I have medical knowledge."

"Tamsin this is Ranon and Gur. Ranon is used to patching us up." Darrogh had clasped her shoulder and she could feel how unsteady his stance was.

"You need to lie down." She wrapped her arm around his waist and led him into the bedroom. When she'd backed his legs against the bed, she pushed him down onto it.

"That is a first." An unfamiliar voice spoke behind her.

She turned to see another warrior. He hadn't come into the house with the first group. Beside him, stood a beautiful blonde-haired woman who was looking at her with raised eyebrows.

"I'm certain you've seen blood before." Tamsin's tone was dry.

"Often." The man's voice held a hint of laughter. "I have never seen Darrogh let a woman touch him."

Tamsin glanced over her shoulder. "Is that a problem?"

"You must be Tamsin Creighton." The woman came up beside her and tried to move her away from the bed. "You have to give Ranon room to work."

Tamsin turned back to Darrogh. Ranon moved to the opposite side of the bed and started to cut through Darrogh's shirt. There was a large hole in his left shoulder that had an ugly puckering around it.

"Tamsin, this is Grace and Partlan. They are mated." Darrogh grimaced as Ranon poked at his shoulder. "Go with them."

Tamsin crossed her arms. "*I stay.*"

She wasn't going to leave Darrogh when he was injured. She didn't care what the new arrivals thought. She was grateful that they had come in time to rescue them, but Darrogh was her mate, and she intended to be at his side.

Darrogh's eyes focused on her. "*I will be fine.*"

Tamsin sat on the edge of the bed.

Partlan left the room, but Grace stayed with her.

Ranon opened a small pack of supplies and pulled out some gauze. He pushed it into the shoulder wound before wrapping a cloth bandage around Darrogh's chest. Other than a quick inhale of breath, Darrogh showed no sign that he was in pain. Ranon moved to the hole in his arm. The bullet had gone straight through. Ranon put a dressing over it.

"You should be able to travel." Ranon put his supplies back into the small pack and shoved it into a large pocket in his jacket. "I will take the bullet out when we are in a safe location."

"Thank you." Tamsin smiled at Ranon before turning to Darrogh. "Can you sit?"

Darrogh groaned as he pushed himself upright.

"I told you I would be fine." His voice was gruff.

"You would not have left me." Tamsin helped him stand.

Once on his feet, Darrogh walked into the main room. There were five Hunters present, including Partlan. They all looked at Darrogh when he appeared and nodded. The bodies of the dead men had been cleared away and the furniture put back in order.

"The site is contained." Partlan was the first to speak.

"I would have killed the rest, but I appreciate your help." Darrogh's voice was strong. "It was dangerous for you to bring Grace."

"She refused to leave my side." Partlan put his arm over Grace's shoulders. "She killed a couple of the Albireons."

"It was a pleasure." Grace must have seen Tamsin's surprised expression because she explained further. "They held me captive in one of their underground labs."

A shiver went through Tamsin. "How terrible."

"Every horrible thing you've heard about the Albireons is true." Grace leaned against Partlan. "I wouldn't be alive if Partlan hadn't saved me."

Darrogh pointed to the other men in the room. "You've met Gur and Ranon. This is Maloc and Turlo. Partlan is the team leader."

Tamsin nodded at the men.

Darrogh took her hand. "This is Tamsin Creighton, my pair bond and mate."

There was a moment's silence and then Grace smiled. "I wondered if that was the case when you refused to leave Darrogh's side."

Partlan shook his head. "I am amazed that you let a woman get close to you."

"It was not easy." Darrogh raised her hand and kissed it. "I fought the pair bond for as long as possible."

The other men slapped Darrogh on the back.

Maloc grinned. "If Darrogh can mate, this gives hope for the rest of us."

Grace gave Tamsin a hug. "Welcome. It's wonderful to have another woman in the group."

"Thank you."

The warmth of acceptance flowed through Tamsin. She knew that the other Hunters who'd been guarding her had accepted her bonding with Darrogh, but she'd been uncertain about how these new Hunters would react.

Darrogh cleared his throat.

"We cannot stay here." Darrogh was in command again. "What are Ardal's orders?"

"He wants you back at the main compound. The Albireon situation has become more serious and he needs to discuss strategy. He cannot leave because Fiona is about to deliver her baby."

"We will head to London first." Darrogh grimaced as he bent to pick up a gun from the table. "What about the Albireon bodies? Are they cleared away?"

"Yes. We came by helicopter. There is not enough room for everyone so Turlo and Maloc will drive the vehicle back."

"Let us go."

Darrogh and Tamsin left the house together. A touch of sadness filled Tamsin at the thought that so much violence had happened where only hours earlier they'd made love.

"*Nothing can destroy our bond.*" She heard Darrogh's words in her head and smiled. He was right of course. Adversity had only made it stronger. She squeezed Darrogh's hand and climbed into the helicopter.

The flight to London, and the ride from the airport to her house in Chelsea Square, took a couple of hours. Tamsin was worried about the bullet in Darrogh's shoulder. Instead of weakening, Darrogh seemed to be getting stronger. By the time they arrived at her house, he seemed out of pain and was using his injured arm freely.

When they arrived, Firbin and Savis were hunched over a computer in her reception room. Tamsin heaved a sigh of relief and threw her bag on the couch. Darrogh went to the computer and leaned over Savis's shoulder to look at the screen.

"What have you accomplished?"

"I have drained all of Albirsion Corporation's assets and the police are aware of Winchester's money laundering." Savis leaned back from the computer. "They arrested Nethercott this morning."

Tamsin's chest tightened. As much as she despised the man's behavior, she still didn't want to see him in jail. He'd been a lousy fiancé, a traitor, and a criminal, but she'd known him most of her life and had no wish to see him destroyed.

"Are the Albireons still watching Tamsin's house?"

"No." Firbin stood. "No one has replaced the ones we killed."

Partlan and his team moved further into the room, followed by Breanon, Jehon, and Kerm.

"I need to get the bullet out of your shoulder before it heals over." Ranon put a large bag on one of the tables. "Is there a room I can do that in?"

"Wouldn't a hospital be better?" Tamsin couldn't hide her dismay.

"We cannot risk it." Darrogh walked to Tamsin, stood behind her, and put his hands on both of her shoulders. "I want to announce that Tamsin has agreed not only to be my mate, but to marry me."

"Good." Savis looked up from his monitor. "I am glad you were able to overcome your doubts."

"So am I." Darrogh pulled her close and kissed her cheek.

Warmth and love flowed through her. Amazing as it seemed, Darrogh was almost back to full strength. He'd told her that Earth had increased their abilities, and faster healing must be one of them. That meant the bullet had to be taken out soon.

"Would one of the bathrooms work for the extraction or would you prefer a bedroom?" Tamsin asked.

"The bathroom would be best." Ranon picked up his bag. "Where is it?"

"Follow me." Darrogh left the room with Ranon.

Tamsin refused to think of all the things that could go wrong with the bullet removal. Instead, she lifted her chin and looked at the rest of her guests. "We have food in the kitchen. Is anyone hungry?"

Darrogh and Ranon returned a half hour later and sat at the dining room table with the rest of the Hunters. Tamsin gave each of them a bowl of soup. There were a few sandwiches left, and a cheese and fruit platter that she passed to the two men.

"Coffee?" Tamsin asked as she offered both of them a mug.

Darrogh nodded and pulled her down onto his lap. He held her close as he ate. His embrace eased her fear about his shoulder. Gradually, Tamsin relaxed and leaned her head against his chest.

"I need to make plans to visit the main compound." Darrogh addressed the rest of the Hunters. "Ardal wants me back there and I will take Tamsin with me. We should go tomorrow, but I want to be certain everything is being monitored here."

"What do you want done?" Firbin put his elbows on the table.

"Someone needs to watch Sir Robert." Darrogh's voice was serious. "The Albireons were willing to risk exposure to kidnap or kill Tamsin. That must mean controlling Creighton's Bank is very important to their plans. Sir Robert needs protection."

"My team can set up surveillance there," Partlan offered. "That will allow your team to continue their work here."

Tamsin straightened away from Darrogh. "My father can be stubborn, but once I've explained what happened at the farm, he'll understand the need for bodyguards."

"I hope he takes it better than you did." Savis's voice was dry.

"I think my father is beyond the age of nightclubs." Tamsin grinned.

Partlan frowned. "I do not understand."

"Tamsin dragged us to a new nightclub every night." Darrogh's voice was gruff. "It was her way of protesting."

Grace laughed. "I would have loved to have seen that."

"The women were throwing themselves at them." Tamsin shook her head as she remembered how ridiculous it had looked. "They kept trying to get them onto the dance floor."

"What are these clubs?" Partlan asked.

"You do not want to know." Darrogh groaned.

Just then the doorbell rang. Tamsin moved to get it, but Darrogh kept a hold on her. He nodded to Breanon who went to assess the situation. She heard her father's voice and stood.

"Have you heard?" Sir Robert walked into the dining room.

"We just arrived back in London." Tamsin guided her father to a chair. He had a grey tinge to his face. "What happened?"

"Winchester Nethercott was found murdered in his holding cell."

Tamsin's breath caught in her throat. Winchester might have done some horrible things, but he didn't deserve to be killed. "Who did it?"

"The police don't know." Her father sat. "They said that their security cameras malfunctioned during the time the murder took place. I came here to be certain you didn't have anything to do with it."

"It is the Albireons." Darrogh clenched his hands. "They are making certain no one speaks."

"Where does that leave us?" Sir Robert asked.

"You need protection." Darrogh's voice was firm. "We were just discussing having a team stationed at your house."

"Tamsin needs to be guarded, not me," Sir Robert said.

"My men and I are watching her." Darrogh gave her father an intense look. "The Albireons are willing to risk discovery in order to get their hands on your bank. You and Tamsin are the key to keeping Creighton's out of Albirsion Corporation control."

Her father leaned back and seemed to debate Darrogh's words for a few seconds before nodding. "You're probably right. If they can't blackmail or threaten me into giving them the bank, then they'll kill me."

"Just like they did with Nethercott." Tamsin's voice was filled with sorrow.

"Sir Robert, meet Partlan and his team of Hunters. This is Ranon, and Gur. Maloc and Turlo are driving Tamsin's car back from Yorkshire." Darrogh turned to Grace. "This is Grace. She is a former FBI agent and Partlan's mate. She will also be joining your security team."

Sir Robert nodded at the men, but hesitated when he turned to Grace. "Does that mean you're Partlan's wife?"

Grace shook her head. "It's more complicated than that. Ask Tamsin to explain it to you one day."

Her father's eyes widened. "What's that supposed to mean?"

"Darrogh asked me to marry him, and I agreed." Tamsin kept her voice steady. "That's all you need to know right now."

Her father's mouth dropped open, and for a second she thought he was going to explode with anger. Instead, he looked at her and then at Darrogh, before nodding. "It's about time you married."

Tamsin exhaled the breath she'd been holding.

Her father's blessing wasn't necessary, but it made life easier.

Darrogh must have sensed how worried she was because she felt a wave of calm being sent her way. She walked over to Darrogh and let him pull her close. Everything was perfect. Being bonded with Darrogh was more than she had ever hoped for. Not only had she found a love that was true and honest, she had found a man that she connected to physically and spiritually. She was filled with happiness and joy.

Now, the only thing left was to meet the rest of Darrogh's unit and their mates.

Chapter 27

Darrogh walked into the compound headquarters with a sense of trepidation.

In the past, he had never considered how his warrior lifestyle would affect anyone else. Now he had Tamsin to consider. Even though he had explained that their lives would be different from what she was used to, he still did not believe that she would remain with him. She came from a background of luxury. A life spent in hiding would be a hardship for her.

"I can accept anything as long as we are together." Tamsin's voice was soft with reassurance.

"You are reading my thoughts."

"And your body language." Tamsin reached up and kissed his cheek. "The only thing I care about is staying with you. You told me that the other Hunters understood that mates cannot be separated."

"True." Darrogh forced himself to relax. "I do not want you to suffer because you have chosen me for your mate."

"We are a pair bond." Tamsin's voice was reasonable. "To deny the bond would be a physical pain to both of us. That would be misery."

"You will have to sacrifice everything to be with me."

"I can do that." Tamsin stopped walking and forced him to turn and look at her. "Are you doubting my commitment?"

A surge of love sent from Tamsin, flowed through him.

He straightened his shoulders. "No. I wish I had more to offer."

"You are all I need."

Darrogh inhaled a quick breath as they continued to walk from the SUV to the compound. He trusted in Tamsin's love and that was all that mattered. The details of their lives would work out the way they were meant to.

The door was opened by Selena Duarte, Catal's mate. "You must be Tamsin. Everyone has been anxious to meet you. I am Selena."

Darrogh followed Tamsin inside. The main area was large and open, with a fireplace in the center, and couches and chairs scattered through the room. Beyond that, were two hallways and the kitchen and dining area. Waiting in the central space was Ardal, the leader of their unit. He looked exhausted, but happy.

Darrogh guided Tamsin into the room. "Ardal, this is Tamsin Creighton, my mate."

"It is an honor to meet you." Ardal gave a slight bow of his head. "To learn that Darrogh had found a pair bond was good news. Darrogh is a skilled and valiant warrior."

Tamsin leaned close to Darrogh. "That doesn't surprise me. Despite my foolishness, Darrogh found and rescued me. The only reason I'm alive today is because of him."

"He has excellent instincts."

Darrogh was uncomfortable receiving such commendations. A Hunter fought and followed orders because it was his duty. He did not expect rewards. Knowing that he lived and died with honor was praise enough.

"Your timing is perfect." Ardal grinned. "Fiona just delivered our daughter this morning."

"Are they okay?" Tamsin's voice was filled with concern.

"Perfect. Kimi has experience with delivery and she also brought one of the midwives from her tribe to help."

"Kimi is Niail's mate," Darrogh explained. "She is a member of the Blackfeet tribe."

"Have you named the baby?"

"Oriana." Ardal's voice was filled with pride. "A golden child."

"That's beautiful."

"Would you like to meet Fiona and the baby?" Selena asked.

"Can I?" Tamsin did not hide her eagerness.

"Fiona has been anxious to welcome a new woman into our group." Selena led Tamsin out of the room and down one of the hallways.

Darrogh turned to Ardal. "You have heard about the Albireon attack."

Ardal nodded. "It concerns me that they were so bold."

"We need a plan to deal with them." Darrogh was focused on military concerns now. "They have infiltrated this planet at every level. They are close to their goal of domination and then the destruction of Earth."

"I have heard from Eogan."

Eogan was a fellow Hunter who had been stranded on Earth and held in captivity for over thirty years. He had been instrumental in aiding Partlan and Grace to escape from the Albireons at the Pine Gap facility in Australia. Because of the interference from the underground military base, Eogan had been unable to mind connect with the other Hunters.

"He has escaped?"

"Yes." Ardal's tone was serious. "He is in Turkey. That is a complicated and dangerous region."

"We need to go to him immediately." Darrogh did not hesitate. "Eogan is a brother and needs our help."

"Agreed." Ardal's voice was firm. "I have sent more Hunters to meet him. They will help in all ways possible."

"What about me?" Darrogh frowned. "You will be here with Fiona and the baby. I am second in command. Should I not go also?"

"You are needed elsewhere." Ardal clasped Darrogh on the shoulder. "I want you to return to London with your mate and live in plain sight of everyone. There will be no secret that you have mated with a human and the Albireons will do everything in their power to sabotage you."

"What is your plan?"

"Tamsin is a wealthy woman and has access to many influential people." Ardal lowered his voice. "Make your presence felt."

"We are to act as bait?"

Ardal shook his head. "You are a distraction. Savis thinks that he will be able to destroy the Albireon computer systems very soon. He needs more time."

Darrogh frowned. He was unused to the ways of the lifestyle that Tamsin lived, yet this would allow her to remain in her world. She would not have to sacrifice anything to be with him. It would be dangerous, though.

"Will you be able to do that?" Ardal's voice was doubtful. "I know that I am asking you to put your mate at risk, but it is necessary in order to defeat the Albireons."

At that moment, Tamsin came back into the room. "What kind of risk."

"I have a plan that involves you," Ardal said. "I intended to ask your permission before finalizing the arrangements."

"No problem. What are we supposed to do?"

"I want you to live your life as normal in London. Be very public about your connection with Darrogh. Let the Albireons know where you are."

"So you want us to taunt them? To rub it in that they didn't succeed in taking over my father's bank?"

"I want them to focus their energies on following you." Ardal leaned back against a table. "It is a great risk and one that I am certain Darrogh will not want you to take."

Tamsin shrugged. "I'm assuming you have activities elsewhere that you don't want them to know about."

"Yes."

"Darrogh will be with me?"

"As will Kerm, Firbin, Jehon, Breanon and Savis."

"A full team." Darrogh nodded. "I will be able to protect Tamsin better that way."

"I would not ask if it were not important for us to gain access to their other facilities. Savis needs more time." Ardal stood. "I understand if you need time to discuss this."

"It sounds perfect to me. I'd be delighted to help out." Tamsin's voice rose with excitement. "Just think, we can have a huge society wedding. I bet even the Duke and Duchess of Cambridge will come."

Ardal left the two of them alone.

Tamsin grabbed Darrogh's hand. "My father will be happy to know that I'm finally going to take an interest in the bank too."

"Is that wise?" Darrogh's tone was doubtful.

"We will be hiding where all of the world can see us. As long as we stay in the public eye, it will be too risky to attack us." Tamsin grinned. "It's wonderful."

"I will have to be with you at all times." Darrogh did not share Tamsin's enthusiasm. He could not deny that it would be harder for the Albireons to kill them if the whole world was watching.

Tamsin leaned closer. "That's what makes it so wonderful. Just think of all the bonding we can do."

Darrogh almost missed a step. He caught himself just in time and pulled Tamsin into his arms. "You are teasing me."

She nodded. "I'm ecstatic to think that we'll be living in London. I have a house big enough for several children and now that I know that Hunters can have children I'm going to want as many as possible."

Tamsin put her arm around his waist and looked up at him with a smile. "Just think, I might be pregnant now."

Panic rose in his chest.

Tamsin stood on her tiptoes and kissed his cheek. "Don't worry. I'll wait until you can handle it. A warrior such as yourself should be ready in a couple of years I would imagine."

"I do not know anything about children."

"Now's your chance to learn." Tamsin walked with him to Fiona's room. "You have to see how adorable Oriana is."

Darrogh was not certain about adorable. The baby's face looked wrinkled and red. He could not deny that Fiona was beaming. Ardal was standing at her side, looking down at the two of them with adoration and pride. Change had never been good for Darrogh. He would have to trust in Tamsin and his fellow Hunters. So far this planet had given them many gifts. Having children was one of them.

Darrogh cleared his throat.

Fiona and Ardal both looked at him.

"I must apologize for my behavior when you were first bonded." Darrogh lifted his chin. "I thought the only way to survive on this planet was to keep things as they had been in the past. I was wrong."

"You are one of the greatest warriors to have ever lived. No Hunter has ever been decorated as often as you or survived as many battles." Ardal looked at him. "I have always respected your opinion and trusted you to do what is best."

"Thank you." Darrogh was humbled by his leader's words of praise.

"I think you did remarkably well considering that you had never been with women until you crashed on my farm." Fiona kissed the baby's forehead. "I wasn't easy to deal with either. I feared men, and all of a sudden, I was surrounded by a unit of Hunters. I didn't react well either."

"You were to be obeyed." Darrogh could not excuse his actions so easily. "I did not understand your connection with Ardal before."

"It is difficult to appreciate it until you have pair bonded." Ardal reached down and took the baby from Fiona's arm. "Having Fiona, and now, Oriana, has taught me more about what being a Hunter is than all of the tenets of the Sacred Code.

It was true.

Until he had bonded with Tamsin, he was only following orders.

Now he had a purpose and peace.

In his years of fighting, he had never dreamed that such a thing was possible. All he had expected was to die an honorable death. Now, he wanted to stay alive so that he could protect Tamsin. She had shown him that there was more to life than just battle and survival. There was hope and love.

THE END

Author's Note

Our world is held together by many bonds, whether it is communication links, cultural similarities or trade agreements. If there is a breakdown, or misunderstanding in any of these areas, the results can be far-reaching. In some cases, it could lead to conflict between nations, and war.

We are also interconnected by our economies and financial institutions. With countries dependent on borrowing money from banks, and central banks using interest rates to help stimulate growth, there is a potential for a spiral of collapse to be created. If interest rates are low, then there's the risk that banks won't be making enough profit to finance personal, business, or government demands. This would result in a slowing of the economy and quite possibly another reduction in interest rates by central banks. The cycle could potentially repeat itself until the flow of money is stopped, and the collapse of international economies is seen world-wide.

The failure of banking institutions and national economies could trigger world collapse and chaos. If there were an alien threat bent on controlling our world, banks would be one of the first areas for them to target.

About the Author

Cynthia Clement is an award winning author who spent most of her childhood with her nose in a book. She began writing stories in her teens, but it wasn't until her forties that she took her writing seriously.

She enjoys ghost hunting, the paranormal, reading and collecting books, quilting, gardening, and great conversation. She has a BSc in Biology, and a BA in Anthropology and recently graduated from nursing.

Cynthia believes in second chances, exploring new ideas, and bringing the impossible to life. Her novels, whether contemporary, historical, or science fiction, all focus on love, honor, and intrigue.

She lives in Northern Ontario with her husband of thirty-two years, her teenage son, and two dachshunds.

Website: www.cynthiaclement.com

Books by Cynthia Clement

Science Fiction

aHunter4Hire series
aHunter4Rescue
aHunter4Saken
aHunter4Life
aHunter4Ever
aHunter4Trust

Historical

Caldern Family
The Seduction of Sarah
The Seduction of Madalyn

Novellas
Pleasuring Emily
Christmas Kisses

www.ingramcontent.com/pod-product-compliance
Lightning Source LLC
Chambersburg PA
CBHW031344170626
46807CB00002B/816